NAKED TO THE NIGHT

NAKED TO THE NIGHT

K. B. Raul

Gay Sunshine Press
San Francisco

ISBN 0-917342-20-8

Gay Sunshine Press Inc.
P.O. Box 40397
San Francisco, CA 94140
Illustrated catalogue of titles available for $1 ppd.

1

H E SLAPPED HIM HARD ON THE CHEEK, and under its harsh stinging impact and unexpected violence, Rick Talbot reeled back, stumbled against the chair and fell. Over him stood his burly stepfather, glaring menacingly, his mouth reeking of liquor.

The noise brought Rick's mother to the room. "Why do you have to torture that poor kid?" she shrieked, and tried to help Rick get up.

"You stay out of this," her husband shouted, pushing her back into the small living room and closing the door. "Get up, you no-good bum. I know you got paid today, so pay me your keep," he shouted, bending to hit Rick again. But Rick was nimble, and he dodged the man, got up and sneaked out while his swaggering stepfather tried to catch him.

"Come back, come back," his mother shouted as he darted out of the house into the street.

Rick's eyes welled up with tears, and his cheeks were still smarting from the slap he had received. His body trembling, he walked on aimlessly until he reached the main street of Clinton, Iowa. He stopped for a minute, but there were too many people and he did not want to run into anyone he knew, so he walked hurriedly on towards the park, where he knew he could sit in a quiet, dark corner by himself.

He knew, as he walked on, that he could no longer live in that hell-hole of a place he called home. His mother had married about four years ago, on the same day John F. Kennedy got inaugurated, as she never tired of telling him, and after a year or so his stepfather had turned his full hatred on him, for no apparent reason. For the past six months the situation had worsened, and there was not a single day that Rick could recall when he had not been brutally treated. His burly stepfather had lost his job at the corn factory as maintenance man. He had been drunk on the job, and his carelessness had resulted in a fire causing considerable damage to life and property. Since then the old man had drifted from job to job, unable to hold on to one for more than a couple of weeks. His joblessness had only increased his consumption of liquor and his cruelty toward Rick. Rick wondered why his mother had married again, what she had seen in this man. His mother was a mousy woman herself, timid and rather weak, who took commands, and constantly wept when things got bad.

Rick was in high school, and during school he used to work in the evenings at the local grocery store as a check out boy for a couple of hours every day. When summer came like it was now, he worked at the town swimming pool as a life guard. But what he made, his stepfather demanded, and his mother always intervened by saying, "Give it to him, baby, give it to him. Let's have some peace in the home."

But there never was any peace, and as he approached the park Rick knew there was not ever going to be peace. He walked towards the end of the park, swept the few pieces of paper and dirt on one of the stone benches and sat down. He let his tears flow unashamedly, uninhibitedly, as though to find some relief from the inner torment of mind and body.

He heard the stroke of seven from the tower clock, and since it was summer, there was still light. It was so quiet here, and he decided he would never go back. But where could he go? Clinton was not a big place. He could not just leave home and go stay in a room of his own. He had to leave town, go away, far away, far, far away. But where? He had never been out of this town. He was a stranger to the world outside.

He was nineteen now, and he was not sure what he wanted to be, or what career he should pursue in life. Of course his secret desire was to be a movie star, but he knew it was a crazy idea. He had appeared in a few high school plays, and in one of them he had impressed his teacher, who had said, "Not bad, Rick, not bad." But more satisfying than the teacher's compliment had been the pat on his ass by Jim O'Neal. Jim, the slim, supple bodied blue eyed blond, had been the high school all-American football star. He had gone to Chicago for a couple of years and returned to Clinton to become the local disc jockey. He was the very personification of the local boy who makes good and returns to serve the community. So when Jim came backstage, congratulated all the actors, and praised Rick in particular by saying, "You were good, fellah. Good," and then patted Rick's ass and drew him close and hugged him, Rick shivered with goose-pimples. He was tongue-tied and could hardly say, "thank you."

Since then, Rick had been stage struck, but was also too embarrassed to confess openly his desires to be a movie star. I should have followed it up, thought Rick as he sat on the bench. I should have acted in a few more plays, but then I couldn't because I had to work in the evenings and couldn't afford time for rehearsals. I should at least have followed up by becoming friends with Jim O'Neal. He took out his wallet and opened it, pulling out a newspaper clipping with a picture of Jim. It was creased and worn, but Rick still got excited when he saw this picture. He had cut it out from the local newspaper soon after Jim had patted and praised him, and had treasured it as a hero's picture—for Jim *was* his hero.

Even now he remembered how he used to crowd into the locker room after each ball game to catch a glimpse of Jim stripped to his waist and streaming with sweat. Rick could never forget that one particular view he had had of Jim after that crucial ball game with Marshall Town High. Clinton had been beaten badly. All of Clinton seemed to have crowded into the locker room area to show sympathy and support for their home team in its hour of defeat. So thick was the crowd that Rick had not been able to glimpse Jim. He had patiently staked out a spot at the far end of the row of lockers, where it was dark, where he knew Jim would be visible when he came to get dressed. Rick was amply rewarded for his patience. Jim was the last to emerge from the shower, his head bowed, his superb golden body all nude and wet. He looked even more exciting in this posture of defeat, very vulnerable and desirable. Had he forgotten his towel? Rick had wondered, seeing the rivulets of water still trickling down Jim's body. He held his breath as Jim approached his locker, took out a large bright yellow towel and dried himself.

That image of his hero, of this blond blue eyed gladiator: the splendid broad chest with the armorplate pecs, the flat washboard stomach, the firm, round, melon buttocks, the thick cock and low hanging egg size balls, had sent shivers of indescribable feelings in Rick. It was an image that remained forever etched in Rick's memory.

Sitting in the park now, he cupped his crotch and pressed his thighs close, as the memory of Jim came back to him. He remembered how he had sat on that rickety stool in the locker room *that* day, long after Jim had eased into his dungarees, sneakers and sweat shirt and left. Rick had walked up to Jim's locker and had found it half open. He had looked inside. On one of the doors was taped a newspaper color photo of one of the cheerleaders. On a hook was Jim's wellworn and sweaty jockstrap. Rick had taken it, sniffed it, and was about to stuff it into his hip pocket when he heard the cough of the janitor. He had fumbled, and the jockstrap had fallen to the floor. Afraid of being caught, Rick had tiptoed out of the locker room area and the gym.

That night Rick had experienced a very erotic sensual dream. He was back in the locker room, and there was his gladiator Jim. He was smiling at Rick and stood with his hands on his hips, his cock hard, erect and throbbing, and his cockhead glistening with a pearly drop of glistening cream. Rick had moved forward and Jim had lifted him up and embraced him and had whispered into Rick's ear 'We are secret lovers, Rick. Secret lovers.'

Rick had regretted not having lifted Jim's jockstrap. For several weeks after that day Rick had tried to lift something intimate belonging to Jim, but had not succeeded. He had watched Jim whenever he could, but never admitted even to himself, that he was in love with Jim. In his deepest moments of self reflection, Rick was tormented by thoughts about his own sexual desires. He wondered if he were a homosexual, a fairy, a queer.

Rick put Jim's picture back in the wallet, and wondered if he should call him up, try and see if Jim would help him. Maybe he wouldn't remember him, but still no harm in trying. What would he say? Oh, he'd say that he was Rick, that he had appeared in a couple of plays, one of which had been seen by Jim; and he wanted to pursue a stage career seriously; and if Jim would help him . . .

As though realizing that more thought on the matter might change his mind, Rick hurried to a drugstore and called up the local radio station.

"Mr. O'Neal is not here anymore. He's been in New York for the past few months," the receptionist told him.

"Where in New York?" Rick asked.

"We don't know. But his mother still lives in town. Ask her," the receptionist said, giving Rick the phone number in Clinton.

After giving Jim's phone number in New York, Jim's mother asked, "Are you going to New York?"

"Yes," said Rick, and by saying that he made up his mind to leave Clinton and go to the big city.

He felt better when he came out of the phone booth, for he had now made the decision. Rick figured out that he'd have about seventy to eighty dollars left after paying his bus fare to New York. Then there was just a little over a week's pay coming to him from his work at the swimming pool. He could ask Bob, the pool manager, to send it to him. The thing to do would be to drop a note to Bob from New York and ask him to send it. Rick decided that he would not wait till morning to see Bob personally, take the money and then leave for New York. It would mean he'd have less cash to spend in the big city, but he could always get a job. He was sure that Jim would help a fellow Clinton kid in finding a job. Yeah, no turning back now. The thing to do was to go.

He found out at the local Greyhound Bus depot that there was a bus leaving for Chicago at nine that night, and that he had to change in Chicago to get to New York. He decided to take that. He had very little to take with him. His few shaving things, a toothbrush, a couple of Levis, gym shorts, two well worn jockstraps, a couple of shirts, three jockey briefs, his bright red swim trunks, all of these would fit into his gym bag. The one jacket he had, he could wear.

He still had another hour before the bus left. He walked towards his home. It was dark; there were no lights. In the living room his stepfather had stretched out on the couch. His big, fat, obscene belly hung out over his belt and he was breathing with his mouth wide open. He did not see his mother—maybe she had gone out to her friend's house for a cup-of-coffee weep. She always did this after a storm in the house. In a way, Rick was glad that his mother was away, for she would have made a scene when she knew that Rick was leaving. It would awaken his stepfather to his fury, and he would even probably have locked up Rick.

Rick came out and waited in the park until bus time, for he did not want to be conspicuous sitting in the small bus depot. Ten minutes before the bus left, he bought his ticket, and felt free and relieved as soon as the bus left Clinton.

9

2

AGAINST A SKYBURST OF RED AND GOLD loomed the tall buildings of New York. The bus sped towards the big city, and Rick sat up looking out of the window, nervous and excited.

Noticing the wide-eyed wonder in Rick's eyes, the fellow sitting next to him asked, "First time to the city?"

"Yes," said Rick, still looking out.

"It shows," the fellow said.

Rick did not answer.

"What're you going to do in the big city?"

"See a friend. Get a job," said Rick.

"What kind of job?"

"Just anything, for the present," said Rick, looking at the rather stockily built, blond crew-cut fellow in tight faded Levis and a knit shirt sitting next to him. His eyes were bloodshot, and he needed a haircut. He had gotten on the bus in Chicago.

"Where you from?"

"Clinton," said Rick.

"Where?"

"Clinton, Iowa," said Rick.

"Oh," said the fellow in a voice that did not appeal to Rick.

"Where are *you* from?" Rick asked.

"Me? I'm from all over. Yeah, I go back and forth, back and forth, all over the good, old U.S.A.," the guy said stretching himself. "Yeah, that's what I do. This is my sixteenth or eighteenth, I forget exactly, trip from L.A. to New York. But it's the first time I've taken the bus. Shit, it's tough all over," he added.

"What do you do other times? Drive?" Rick asked.

"Drive?" the fellow laughed. "Yeah, I drive. You can say that. I hitchhike. This time I got as far as Chicago, and for two days I couldn't get out. I got restless. Hell, I said, I picked up a few bucks and bought myself a ticket. I tell you, Chicago was tough. Lots of fresh meat on the streets, tough competition, tough. Real tough."

Rick wanted to ask what the tough competition was, or what the guy meant by lots of fresh meat, but looked out of the window, and tried to ignore the fellow next to him. At around eight-thirty the bus pulled up at the Thirty Fourth Street bus depot. He thought of calling up Jim immediately, but decided to rest, clean up and call him in the morning.

He went up the stairs to the men's room, and as he stood at the urinals, noticed that the fellow next to him was the guy who had been with him on the bus.

"What do you say, we meet again," he said.

Rick did not reply, and did not like the way the guy was staring at his cock. Embarassed, Rick eased his cock back into his tight levis, zipped up and came out.

The fellow followed him down the stairs. "Hey, kid, wait a minute," he said, catching up with Rick. "Boy, you sure are in a hurry. Afraid I'd make a grab at your meat," he added, laughing and putting his hand on Rick's shoulders.

Rick pulled away.

"Listen, kid, where you staying?"

"I don't know," said Rick, hurrying out of the depot.

"Listen. If you've got no place, I know a cheap place where we can sack out. Six bucks a night, three bucks a piece. It isn't the Waldorf, but then we ain't millionaires," he said.

"No thanks," said Rick.

"Hey, listen," the fellow persisted, but Rick moved fast. "I could teach you how to sell that chunk of meat you got," the guy shouted after him.

Rick hurried on. He walked towards the YMCA sign he saw in front of him. The counter was crowded with people, and Rick had to wait for nearly an hour before he got a room.

It was a small but clean room. He stood happily in the room. It was his own, private and free to enjoy. He took a long hot shower, changed into fresh underwear, shirt and Levis and went out.

It was getting cooler outside. He felt refreshed and excited. Although it was getting close to ten-thirty, the streets were as crowded with people as they would be around suppertime in

Clinton. He had his dinner at Bickford's and walked on, aimlessly looking at all the shops and people until he arrived at brightly lit Times Square. Good Lord, he had never seen so many people! And all those movie houses one beside the other, not showing one feature as in Clinton, but two and even three. And what a variety to choose from. And look at that guy over there tossing that dough up in the air to make a pizza. The variety of the streets fascinated him. He walked around for some time, and finally selected a movie house which was showing three features, *Summer Love* with his favorite actor John Saxton, *Rawhide Years*, and *Gunfight at Dodge City,* all for seventy-five cents. He walked in, bought a big bag of popcorn, and sat down to indulge in his favorite pastime.

It was close to three-thirty in the morning when he came out. The streets were still buzzing with people, although there were not the big crowds he had seen before. He walked towards a hotdog stand and bought one. While he was eating, he noticed an old man looking at him intently. He came up to Rick, and smilingly said, "Hi, kid. Want to make a couple of bucks?" But Rick was nauseated by the stench of cigar smoke and beer on the old man's mouth, and it brought back the ugly image of his stepfather. He left immediately to avoid the old man, and dumped his half-eaten hotdog in a garbage can nearby.

In his hurry to get to the Y and sleep, he bumped into a group of four boys all in tight levis and T shirts. "Hello, sweetie," said one. "Where you going in such a hurry?" "Boy, he sure is a cute kid, he sure is," said a big black boy. "That you are, sweetie. Let me take you home and give you a knee trembler blow job," added a slim red haired kid almost reaching out to embrace Rick.

Rick nimbly evaded him and ran.

3

"HE LEFT A FEW DAYS AGO, didn't say where he was moving to, said he'd be back to pick up his mail. Not that he has any," said a lady with a heavy nasal voice, when Rick called Jim's number.

"You know when he'll be back?"

"Couldn't say," she said and hung up.

So Jim was out. Rick decided to stay on in the city, although he hated to admit that trying to find Jim in the city was now practically impossible. He wrote a letter to Bob, asking him to send him the money he had coming to the Y address, and mailed another letter to his mother without giving her his return address.

All he could now do was to try and get a job, get settled and then begin thinking about his future plans. He had paid for his room for a week and had around twenty bucks left. If Bob sent him that money, he could last until he found a job. But the day was hot, and Rick decided that he would take it easy and start looking for a job the next day.

But the sudden new-found freedom and the endless fascinating variety of New York seen from his small-town perspective kept Rick from making any serious attempt in looking for a job. He discovered Coney Island, and since swimming was a favorite sport of his, he spent the afternoons on the beach, sunning himself and dipping into the ocean as the spirit moved him. His lunch consisted of a hotdog and a hamburger washed down with coke. Returning from the beach, he would sleep at the Y after reading film magazines which he started buying from an old second-hand magazine store near Times Square. His appetite for the plush world of movie stars increased after reading the juicy columns written for a gullible public by seasoned writers of the fantasy world of Hollywood.

Late nights would find Rick scanning the signs on Forty Second Street, selecting the movies he would attend to lose himself once again into the world of dreams and grandeur.

There was no reply from Bob, and no money either. A week later Rick found that his room rent was due the following day. All he had was two bucks and some change.

He decided to look for a job. Interested as he was in the movies, Rick thought it would be a good idea if he could get an usher's job in one of the innumerable movie houses in and around Times Square. He began asking at each one, but found nothing until he reached the seventh theatre.

"Go see the manager in the basement. He might have something," said the old, heavily made-up lady at the ticket counter.

Rick knocked on the door of the manager's room, and heard a loud voice asking him to come in.

Seated in front of a large table was a muscular clean shaved person. His smooth round scalp gleamed under the light above him, and his biceps seemed to burst out from his white T-shirt.

"Close the door, kid, what can I do for you?" he asked looking at Rick intently.

"Yes sir," said Rick, closing the door. "I'm looking for a job."

"What kind?"

"Maybe an usher or something."

"You ever worked as an usher?"

"No."

"Where you from?"

"Clinton, that's in Iowa."

"Nice fresh farm boy, huh?"

Rick smiled.

"You in any kind of trouble?"

"Trouble?"

"Yeah. Trouble. You know, running away from something. Lot of kids do that. Get into trouble back home, then hitchhike to New York. Anything like that?" he asked, surveying Rick very closely.

"No, nothing like that, sir, nothing at all."

"How old are you?"

"Twenty," Rick lied.

The manager stared at him. "Turn around," he ordered.

Rick obeyed.

The manager got up from his chair and walked over and circled around Rick examining him. Rick looked downward, scratching the carpet floor with his toes.

"Yeah, I could use a guy like you. Can you work nights, the late shift?"

"Any time at all, sir, any time at all," said Rick eagerly.

"If it's too late, or you're too tired, I can even find a bed for you here. Come around at eight tonight, come see me then. We'll talk about pay then," he said giving Rick's shoulder a big squeeze.

"Thank you, sir, thank you," said Rick, feeling very happy as he came out of the room, closing the door behind him.

That was a good break thought Rick. It would, of course, be some time before he got paid, and he had to renew his room and he needed money to live till then. Maybe he could ask the manager for an advance. He'd somehow manage. The good thing was he finally had a job. Maybe Bob might even send his money. He dropped another post card to him.

He spent the afternoon as usual at Coney admiring the bronzed physiques of a few of the guys on the beach and visualised himself as a gorgeous muscleboy. Then he returned to the Y and slept until seven, took a shower and arrived at the movie house a few minutes before eight.

There was a pale, effeminate-looking guy at the refreshment stand. "You're the new usher?" he asked Rick as he was walking in.

"Yeah."

"Your uniform is in the manager's room. Get into it, and go relieve the red haired kid who's on the floor," he said.

"Thanks," said Rick and went down to change.

There was no one in the manager's room. Rick was glad that there was no one. His clothes had all become dirty, and he was just wearing his levis with no underwear. He changed into a rather ill-fitting worn blue uniform with a sickly-looking yellow border on the coat lapels and cuffs, and came out.

He relieved the seedy-looking, red-haired guy, whose hairline seemed to be receding even as Rick watched him.

There was nothing much to do actually. Just walk around, wake up people who tried to sleep or were sleeping, prevent people from smoking or taking a nip from a bottle, and chores similar to that. The theatre was not crowded, and Rick got a chance to see half of *Battle Cry* and all of *Alexander the Great,* with cartoons and newsreel thrown in.

The last of the moviegoers left at 3 A.M. and Rick went down the basement to change and leave. He needed some money, and blamed himself for not checking to see if the manager was in to ask for a loan or an advance. He thought of coming by early next day before noon, to get some so as to renew his room by noontime. He was therefore pleasantly surprised when he went inside the manager's room and found the manager seated at the table wearing a red silk robe.

Rick was glad to see him. Now he could ask him for some money. Yet at the same time he wished he were alone for he felt embarrassed to change in front of the manager.

But the manager seemed to be concentrating hard on the papers in front of him, and Rick went over to the couch to pick up his clothes to change into them. He quickly undressed, and as he was struggling to ease into his tight levis with his shoes on, the manager looked up and asked, "How did it go?"

"Fine," said Rick, still struggling to get his feet into those narrow leg openings.

"Take it easy, kid," the manager said, as he saw Rick in a hurry. "Listen, why don't you stay right here? Sack out on the couch," said the manager rising.

"Thanks, but I think I'll go back to the Y," said Rick. He lost his balance and fell to the floor.

The manager came out from behind the desk and loomed over Rick. "Hey, you're a nice looking kid, you sure are. Big meat you got there."

Rick was embarrassed. He tried to get up and the manager helped him. He put his hand on his shoulder, "Listen, kid. Come over here, let's sit down. Leave those stupid jeans. I like kids this way," he said and caressed Rick's naked buttocks.

Rick pulled away. "No, it's getting late now," he said.

"Late? So what? Come on, let's have some fun. I'll take good care of you. I'm hot for you, baby, real hot. See," the manager said and parted his bath robe. He was stark naked and Rick saw the thick hard erection, like a burst sausage.

"No. Please let me go," said Rick moving backwards, away from the approaching manager.

"Stop playing around. Come on," said the manager, dropping his bath robe and advancing towards Rick, catching him by the wrist.

"Let me go, let me go," cried Rick.

The manager was twisting Rick's wrist.

"I'll scream for help. I'll call," Rick cried out in pain.

"Call for help? Who? The cops? You whining son of a bitch. You faggot! You think anyone can hear you? And even if they heard you,

I'd say you're new here, just started today, and you were trying to steal. In half a minute you'd be locked up."

The manager hurled Rick onto the couch. As Rick tried to get up, the muscular manager struck him hard on the face, turned him over, parted his cheeks and brutally raped him.

4

RICK SPENT A VERY RESTLESS NIGHT and had fallen asleep during the early hours of the morning around seven. The maid knocked on his door at noon and told him that he had to either renew his room or check out. Not having money to renew, he collected all his things and went to the washroom. After a shower, he checked out, without the least idea as to where he was going or what he was going to do.

Carrying his gym bag, he walked Forty Second Street and went to Bickford's for coffee. He sat absentmindedly thinking about the gruesome event of the previous night. He didn't really care as to what happened to him now, after last night's ritual of violence. Maybe he should have yielded to the manager, at least gotten some money that way. Hell, he wasn't going to think about it any more.

"Ah, so you're here. I told you I'd see you."

Rick looked up and found that the speaker was none other than the fellow who had been with him on the bus. Rick did not speak.

"Mind if I join you?" the fellow asked.

"I don't care," said Rick.

The fellow left his copy of *The Daily News* on the seat opposite Rick's chair, and went to get a cup of coffee.

"So, how's New York treating you?" he asked when he came back and sat down.

Rick did not answer. The fellow did not pursue the question further but started reading the paper and drinking his coffee. He looked much better than he did on the bus. His eyes were not so bloodshot, his black T-shirt was clean, and his wheat colored dungarees were new. He had also had a haircut. Rick looked at him for a minute or so, and as an answer to his earlier question said, "I don't like New York. Not one bit."

The fellow did not lift his head from the paper he was reading, but said, "Greatest city in the world, boy, yeah, it sure is. The big bright juicy apple. You have to know how to take a bite of it. That's all there's to it."

"Oh, shit. It's a jungle," said Rick spitting out the words.

"Hey, you *are* mad. What happened?" the fellow asked, folding his newspaper. Rick did not answer. "You want a cup of coffee?" the fellow asked. Rick hesitated, but said, "Might as well."

The fellow bought two more cups of coffee, and giving one to Rick said, "Listen, kid, what happened really? You can tell me. Confession's good for the soul, so they tell me. Tell me. I got all the time in the world to listen. I've been through a lot of things myself."

Maybe it was just a touch of sincerity in that voice, or maybe it was the human need to communicate, but Rick poured out his experience to this stranger whom he had only a few days ago detested for his prying, vulgar looks.

"That bloody sonofabitch, God help me, I would have killed him if I had been you!" said the fellow, clenching his fist and showing his anger at Rick's unfortunate experience.

Rick was drawn closer to this fellow by this spontaneous outburst of sympathy and anger.

"What do you plan to do now, kid. By the way, what is your name?"

"Rick."

"Jake's my name. Well, what do you plan to do?"

"Oh, I don't know, and I don't really care."

"Listen, kid, I mean Rick. Shall I tell you what's on my mind?"

"Sure. You're the first person who's ever asked my permission to say what you want to say," said Rick.

"Listen. You're one hell of a good looking kid. Your bright dark eyes, that thick head of brilliant dark hair, movie star face, humpy body. You're fresh, wholesome, clean, just great. And from the glimpse I got of your tool at the bus depot the other day, I'd say you're well hung. I bet you get real humoungous when you get hard. Right?" he said, laughed and patted Rick on the shoulder. He took a sip of coffee and continued. "Take a swing at me if you like, but hear me out first. Okay?"

"Go on," said Rick.

"What I'm trying to say is, with your body and cock, and my street smart instincts, we can team up into a good pair of hustlers. I know this town. I mean, I know it. I can protect you. You see what I mean?"

19

"Not exactly," said Rick.

"Come on Rick, you know what I'm talking about. You're not that dumb. I've been hustling ever since I was sixteen. Now I'm around thirty, maybe a little more, maybe less. Who knows and who cares? I used to be a hunk like you. Real Nordic blond, blue eyes, muscular body, super round firm ass. My best assets. Guys used to go crazy over me. I can tell you stories you've never heard before. Good life, I mean. Plush. I had some movie stars who used to kiss my ass. Literally kiss my ass, worship it. But that's history, right? In this game you grow old fast. You gotta strike it when you're hot and young. Young like you," Jake said sipping his coffee with a nostalgic look.

"But you and me, Rick, I have a hunch we'll strike it. You're gorgeous. You look like that teen-age Italian movie star, hell, I can't remember his name, but honest, you do look like him. We'll play around here for some time, then when it gets cool, we'll go to Florida, then to L.A. and lie on the beach. You get bronzed in the California sun, pump iron, wear a real skimpy bikini, show off your balls and cock, and some talent scout or agent sees you, snaps your picture, and bingo you're a movie star," said Jake scripting a scenario of fantasy and illusion.

Rick laughed, his first relaxed laugh.

"I'm not kidding. You can make it, Rick. It's happened before. I could have made it, but I blew it. You can learn from my mistakes. Others have made it. I can give you dozens of examples. I know some kids not half as good-looking as you who have hit the jackpot. I've made a lot of mistakes as a hustler, but I've learned my lessons. If you team up with me, I'll show you the ropes. What do you say?" Jake asked, his arm on Rick's shoulder.

"You mean end up as a male whore?" asked Rick.

"A male model is how you call yourself."

"But still a whore."

"If you want to put it that way."

"There's no other way of putting it."

"So what do you say? Sure, suppose you don't become a movie star—we can still team up, make up some dough, then hit the road to L.A. or some place, open up a nice bar, or some such thing. I got connections. I'll say one thing, Rick, I'm clean. No prison record or anything like that. Yeah, sure I've rolled a couple of drunks now and then after they've given me a grope, but nothing else," said Jake, lighting a cigarette and offering it to Rick.

Rick declined.

Neither spoke for a few minutes.

"I know nothing about all this," Rick said quietly. "I came here with hopes. Now I'm broke, hungry, been raped and don't know a goddamn place to go. And after what happened last night, nothing worse could happen to me except get killed. So what have I got to lose?"

"Does this mean we're in business?" asked Jake.

"But I won't get fucked, that's for sure."

"You don't have to, Rick, you don't have to. Guys will beg you to fuck them. With what you've got, if I package you right, and believe me I will, you'll have guys drooling over you. Just unzip and get hard and let a guy blow you. Close your eyes and count the money you're going to get. Okay?"

"But I've never done this kind of thing before."

"That adds to your charm. Don't worry. I'll give you all the tips you need. I'm an expert. I can write a book about how to hustle. Okay? Let's shake on it, pal," said Jake, offering his hand. They sealed their partnership.

"How much moola you got?" Jake asked.

"Huh?"

"Moola, bread, money?"

"Oh, a couple of bucks, maybe less."

"I got three bucks. I've paid the room rent for tonight. We can both shack up in the same place. Another fifty cents, I can ask the old guy to allow us both. So that leaves together about five bucks. It's early now, but we can still start. Let's go back to my hotel room, leave your gym bag, come back around five or five-thirty. I know quite a few guys who pick up some fun on their way from work, for a quickie before they go home to their ugly wives. We could make a few bucks that way," planned Jake.

"Listen, Jake, not today. Okay?" said Rick.

"How about tonight?"

"No, not today. I'll start from tomorrow. Okay?"

"Okay, okay. What'll you do now?"

"Let's go up to your place. I'll sack out for some time, then go see a movie or something."

"I ain't coming to no movie. We'll go to my room. You sack out, I'll come back and prowl. I know a guy who comes around this part of the week and with no sweat off my back I can easily make five or ten. He's a balls freak, just sucks on my balls. If I shave my balls, then

21

I can get a bit more. It all depends on his mood and time," said Jake.

"I can see there's much to learn by the way you talk," Rick said.

"No problem. You'll learn fast. I can tell," said Jake.

They got up and left, and as they were coming out, an old guy brushed his hand against Rick and said, "Can I buy you a coffee?"

"My friend don't drink coffee today, but I do," said Jake.

"I like your friend," said the old man.

"Get lost," growled Jake and came out of the cafeteria.

Jake stayed in one of those dark, dingy, dollar-fifty-a-day hotels where you climbed four flights of creaking stairs to a cubicle of a room.

"Hey, pops," said Jake to the man at the desk at the foot of the stairs.

The man peered from his thick eyeglasses and said, "What now?"

"Listen, here's another fifty cents for my buddy from California who's going to stay with me," said Jake handing over a fifty-cent piece.

"Fifty? Since when is it fifty? It's a buck and you know it," growled the man.

"A buck? What's this, the Plaza or something? Oh, come on pops, give us kids a break," said Jake.

"A buck. I just work here," the old man said.

"Listen pops, you take fifty cents and I'll arrange it so you get to see my buddy nude in the shower, or even watch him take a piss. His cock, it's out of this world," said Jake.

"Oh, yeah?" the old man said.

"You watch," said Jake and the man took the fifty cent piece.

"But why did you stand me up last night?" the old man asked.

"Sorry, pop, I got tied up last night. But I'll make it up to you. I was so pooped last night I wouldn't have been much good to you anyway. Okay?" said Jake.

Jake put his arms around Rick's waist and they went up the narrow stairs.

"You know, Jake, you ought to check with me before you offer me," said Rick.

"You mean the old guy? Oh, don't worry about that. I've been promising him erotic fantasies ever since I've been in and out of this place. He's a real weirdo. He's into golden showers."

"Golden showers?" Rick asked as they started to climb the four rickety old flights of stairs.

"He likes to be pissed on, Rick. Just stand above him and stream out your fresh warm golden shower. Comprende?" Jake said and hugged Rick.

They reached the fourth flight and came to a room at the end of a dim corridor, next to the washroom which had no door.

"Don't you lock it?" Rick asked as Jake opened the door with a push.

"Lock? No locks here. There's nothing to steal," said Jake shutting the door after them.

It was a real narrow room with a double bed and no other furniture. There were two windows, one stuck down and pasted over with newspapers and the other opening out to a wall on the other side. It was a hot oven of a box, and rather dark until Jake pulled the greasy string and the yellow, sickly-looking bulb lighted up from the top of the ceiling.

"Whew, it's hot," said Rick, taking off his jacket.

"It's not so bad in the early morning, around three or four. That's when I come in to catch some shut eye," said Jake.

Rick was looking around.

"Want to stay or come out?" Jake asked.

"I think I'll stay."

"Okay, see you later," said Jake and left.

Rick sat on the bed, then fell back, but got up and stripped nude, and sweated freely. He put out the light and stretched out naked on the bed. He rolled over, hugged the limp pillow, buried his head in it, and gradually dropped off to sleep.

It was slightly cooler when he woke up. He was wet with sweat. He walked naked into the dirty little washroom next door to the room and began to throw cold water upon himself from the leaking faucet. He got back to the room, pulled up the dirty bed sheet and dried himself with it. Putting on his levis and T-shirt, he left the hotel, ate a hotdog and washed it down with coke and began to scan the movie houses to decide what he would see. He decided on *High School Confidential* and *Running Wild,* and went in.

He was asleep when Jake came in, and woke up with a start when he felt a naked body next to him.

"Easy, baby, easy. It's only me, your buddy Jake. I'm not going to hurt you. I promise I won't," said Jake putting his hand on Rick's naked chest.

Rick sat up.

Jake put his hand on Rick's back and said, "Rick."

"Yeah?"

"Lie down, honey."

Rick did not answer.

"Rick, baby. Come. Let me teach you," said Jake, his voice soft and husky with desire. He gently pushed Rick back on the bed. Rick was trembling. "Baby, you're shaking like a leaf. Nothing to fear, honey, nothing at all," said Jake caressing Rick's thighs and moving up to stroke his balls. Rick tensed. Jake bent over and kissed Rick's nipples which grew hard. He sniffed the moist armpits of Rick, inhaling the rich musky odor. Jake's fingers stroked Rick's cock which grew to its full height and glory. The velvety knob glistened and Jake's tongue lovingly caressed the shaft and the thick veins on it. Rick moaned and whimpered in ecstasy and Jake slowly inserted his middle finger up Rick's tight crack and passionately sucked out his cream as Rick cried out.

5

I T WAS JAKE WHO WOKE UP FIRST in the morning. The sharp shaft-like sunlight shot through the window. He didn't feel that tremendous sense of loneliness that he felt every morning when he woke up, for he saw Rick lying beside him. He smiled and gazed at Rick, sleeping nude and relaxed. He sure is a good looking stud, thought Jake. His eyes took in the handsome, well-tanned face; the thick dark eyebrows; the thick dark black hair; the broad chest; the well formed pecs; the slim torso; the lean, vigorous flanks; the muscular thighs. Jake gently pushed back the hair from Rick's forehead, bent down and kissed his full lips. Rick woke, looked at Jake and smiled, then stretched his body vigorously, almost lifting it up from the bed. It was a graceful gesture in which the beauty and virility of Rick's lean young body revealed itself. Rick's cock thickened with the glory of the early morning erection. Jake trembled with desire as he watched. He passionately embraced Rick, Rick playfully resisted, but they kissed each other as Jake's palm cupped his big low hung balls. Then Rick released himself. "Hey, let's not get all excited again. We can't stop," he said and leaped out of bed.

"Sure, baby, sure, got to save some for the customers," said Jake, observing Rick's firm round buttocks, as Rick eased into his levis.

"Just a few more pounds, honey, and you'll be an adonis. Irresistible," said Jake, getting up and looking under the bed for his black shorts.

"Yeah, when we start making some dough then I'll live on red, juicy steaks all the time," said Rick, putting on his T-shirt.

"You're the one to make money, baby, not me," said Jake, stepping into his black shorts.

Rick smiled and said, "Looks like you bought some sexy new shorts."

"This guy that sucked me off last night insisted I wear black shorts. I said, 'buy me a pair.' And he did. Rather tight though," said Jake pulling at his crotch.

"Looks nice on you," said Rick.

"You can have it, baby, if you want it. By the way, did I teach you good?" Jake asked.

"Teach?"

"Yeah, last night, here in this school," said Jake, pointing to the bed.

"Oh, that."

"What did you like best on the menu?" asked Jake, drawing on his dungarees.

"Oh, come on," said Rick, blushing ever so slightly at the lewd suggestions in Jake's speech.

"Don't be shy with words, baby. Some guys like dirty talk while you fuck their mouths or ass. I mean it, well you'll learn. You're a man, baby, all man. Real macho with that cock you got. I've never seen anything that thick, that hard and that strong," said Jake.

"You mean that?" Rick asked.

"Honest. It's the finest meat I've ever seen or felt. It was a joy to suck you, Rick. And I tell you, for a newcomer, man, you fuck like a heavy duty non-stop construction worker. It was some super fuck you gave me, baby," said Jake rubbing his buttocks.

Rick smiled, hit Jake playfully on his biceps and said, "Okay, let's go get something to eat. I'm hungry after all that . . ." His voice trailed off.

"Say it, baby. Say it. After all that, what?" Jake coaxed.

"After all that heavy duty fucking," said Rick.

"There you go. It sounds so damn sexy when you say it. You're a gold mine, baby, a real gold mine," said Jake admiringly.

It was three-thirty in the afternoon when they came out.

"Hell, we sure slept," said Rick.

"Sex is strenuous," said Jake.

They washed up in the washrooms at the Port Authority Bus Terminal and went to Bickford's on Forty-Second Street for breakfast. Jake paid for eggs, bacon and toast and coffee. They split a *Daily News* that someone had left on one of the tables, and read it while they ate in silence.

"That was good. You think you could treat me to another order of whole wheat toast?" Rick asked.

"Sure, baby. Sure," said Jake and went over to get some toast.

"Thanks," said Rick taking the toast. "You must have made some money last night," he added.

"Chicken feed," said Jake lighting a cigarette.

After a few minutes, Rick said, "Well, what do we do now?"

"We gotta do things properly. First thing we gotta get you some new threads," said Jake.

"Clothes? What for. I got enough to wear, besides, you have to take it off anyway," protested Rick.

"Listen, baby, to sell something for the right price, you got to package it properly. Sometimes people go more for the package than the real thing. But with you when you got the jewelry, it doesn't hurt displaying them," said Jake.

"These are okay, Jake . . ."

But Rick was interrupted. "See, see that guy over there," said Jake, looking towards the cafeteria food counter.

"You mean that sailor?" asked Jake.

"Well, he's no more in the navy than I'm in the marines. Anyway, yeah, the guy in them white navy pants," said Jake.

"What about him?"

"Heck, take a look at them tight pants. Look at the way they show off his nice tight round ass, and wait, now look at his crotch. Look at that big basket he's got. God, you can see his balls outlined. See what I mean?"

The sailor, who had turned now, was leaning over the counter and his tight white pants were stretched taut over his melon round buttocks, and the fabric cleaved his cheeks. They were so tight that they revealed the outline of his brief undershorts. When he walked to a table with a cup of coffee and a plate with a Danish, his cap arrogantly perched on his thick curly blond hair, Rick got excited watching the sailor's bulging crotch. The sailor had now become the center of attention in the cafeteria. He slowly sat down straddling a chair. There was restless movement among the crowd in the cafeteria as many a person planned to strike up a conversation with the sailor without making it look too obvious. But a nattily dressed black, without caring a damn as to what others thought, ambled across to the sailor's table and asked him openly for a match. The sailor held out a light.

The black guy sat opposite the table. They were silent for a minute. The black looked around and said rather loudly, "Too many goddamn guys here, let's go to some nice quiet place. Okay? I'll make it worth your while." The sailor did not reply, but just got up and they both left the cafeteria with the black guy putting his hand on the sailor's buttocks.

"But I don't go for those tight pants," said Rick, after the pickup was made.

"That's our uniform, baby. You gotta dress for the job. Can you imagine how your meat would look packaged like that? You'll create a stampede," said Jake and laughed.

"Okay, okay. But where have we got the money for clothes? asked Rick.

"Leave that to me. Come on, let's go," said Jake.

"Where to?"

"Buy some clothes."

They came out and took the subway to Grand Central Station. On the way, Jake told Rick to be very friendly with the guy they were going to meet.

They got out and walked up to a "Togs for the Male" shop on Lexington Avenue. It was a small corner shop, its existence almost hidden by other shops around.

"Hi, Andy, what do you say?" said Jake as he entered.

The rather plump-looking, baldish man at the counter was startled by this, and he nervously said, "Oh, hello."

"What are you doing, Andy?" Jake asked.

"Oh, Jake. It's you! Haven't seen you in a while. Wasn't it about two months ago when you walked in, got a bikini for that cute number you had with you, said you'd be back in the afternoon . . .?"

Jake interrupted him. "Andy, I tell you that cute number proved to be a disaster. I am sorry. But let me introduce my new friend to you. Rick, this is Andy, a real friend. Andy, this is Rick. Fresh from L.A."

"Hi."

"Hi."

"How's business, Andy?" Jake asked.

"Not good. Lots of competition. As you can see I just carry two things in my store, slacks and underwear. Got a few shirts left. When they're sold, that's it," said Andy, his eyes focused on Rick.

"It's tough all over, Andy, tough all over. Listen, my buddy wants a couple of things from you. He's got a very important audition this evening, has to have some fancy duds. So you see, Andy, I bring you business. I never forget you," said Jake, hitting Andy on the back.

"What does he want?"

"A pair of slacks, something sexy under it, maybe a shirt or two.

Rick, you tell Andy what you want. He'll fix you up," said Jake.

"I guess that ought to do it," said Rick.

"What did you have in mind?" Andy asked.

"I guess you know the styles," said Rick.

"You are a very agreeable person," said Andy.

"He's a jewel, Andy. A real jewel," said Jake gripping Rick's arm.

"That's so refreshing to hear. You should see the guys who come in here. They'll try on every slack I've got and then leave without buying a thing. They want something tight to show off, but if they haven't got something in the first place, how can they show off," Andy said, his body quaking with laughter.

"Wait till you see what Rick's got," Andy said, and then when he saw Rick stare at him, he said, "I'm sorry."

"Take a look at what I got. Slacks, I mean," said Andy and laughed. He went over to the slack bar, examined a few and brought back two, a light grey and a midnight blue. "What's your waist size?" he asked Rick.

"Around 29 or 30."

"Well, let's see," said Andy, measuring, "Yeah, you're right. 29 should be nice and snug. Now for the length. He measured Rick from the crotch down, giving a gentle pressure to Rick's crotch, adding, "You don't wear any underwear, do you?"

"He doesn't have to," said Jake and laughed.

"Why don't you try these?" Andy said.

"I prefer the darker one," said Rick.

"Good choice. These have no pockets, very low rise, a four-inch zip, real snug, shows off your buns. Just the thing for someone with your build," Andy explained.

"Where shall I try this on?" Rick asked.

"In front of us, of course," said Andy and seeing the consternation on Rick's face, said, "Just joking. Come, here's the little place where you can strip."

As Rick followed Andy, Jake winked slightly at him.

The dressing room, as it was called, was behind the slack bar, a real small place with a full length mirror, with a green curtain hung in front of the alcove.

Noticing that Andy was still standing in front, with the curtain held apart, Rick hesitated, so Andy dropped the curtain, and allowed Rick to try out his slacks.

The slacks fit him perfect, the fabric clinging to him, sculpturing and molding his body. But it made things rather obvious, he thought. They'd arrest him in Clinton if he walked on the street dressed like this.

"Are they okay?" shouted Andy.

Rick came out.

"Gosh, you leave me breathless," said Andy. Turning to Jake who had come up, he said, "You weren't telling lies about Rick, that's for sure."

"Rick's the best, Andy. The cream of the crop," Jake said.

"I ought to take a size larger," said Rick, examining himself. His thick cock even in its limp stage seemed to be jutting forward under the tight fly of the trousers.

"Of course not. The cuffs need to be fixed. I can do that in no time at all. Loose? Hell, no. There are hundreds of guys, top male models I mean, who'd give anything to have a figure that would look well in these pants. One thing I would suggest," said Andy, feeling Rick gently in the back, "is skimpy underwear. I got a nice sexy Swedish item, made of lycra. Let me show you." He went over and fussed around in several drawers and came out with a bright red bikini.

"Haven't you got that in white?" Rick asked.

"Be bold, wear black or red. Very sexy erotic colors, my dear," Andy said and gave the red bikini to Rick.

Rick went over to the dressing room. The lycra stretch bikini fit him snug and gave definition to his huge cock, enlarging rather than concealing his proportion. When he eased back into his slacks, his basket looked like a clenched fist.

"Just terrific," said Andy, trying to cop a feel.

"Watch your hand, boy. That's expensive merchandise, no free samples," said Jake.

"You should get a nice smart shirt, a sort of a Jack shirt, coming right up to the waist. Let me show you," said Andy, and went to get it.

"Play it cool, Rick," whispered Jake, brushing his hands against Rick's fly.

"This one?" asked Andy, showing a light blue one.

"Any other color?" Rick asked.

"Sorry, this is the only color in your size."

Rick liked his appearance.

"A little trim of your hair in the back, another pair of shoes, some cologne splashed on your hot body, and you'll slay hearts," said Jake. "Andy, when can you get these slacks fixed?"

"In a couple of days," said Andy, looking at Rick.

"Couple of days! We can't wait that long," Jake exploded.

"Rick, when do *you* want it?" Andy asked.

"How about in a couple of hours?"

"Your wish is my command. I'll have it for you in a couple of hours. Go take them off, Rick," said Andy.

After Rick had left, Jake said, "Andy, you gotta give us a couple of days before we can pay."

"Jake, have a heart, I got to live," said Andy.

"Listen," said Jake almost in a whisper, "I'll see that Rick will allow you to feel his meat."

"Feel his meat? I want to suck that cock. I want to get fucked by that stud. The full treatment and I'll give the clothes free. I'll even buy him a pair of shoes and a bottle of cologne. That's fresh meat, Jake. The best you've brought so far," enthused Andy.

"You leave it to Jake. Listen, Andy, you think you can give me five bucks? I'll pay you back, promise," said Jake.

"Promises, promises," said Andy and cupped Jake's crotch.

"For ten bucks you can give me a quickie suck," Jake said.

"My mouth is salivating for Rick. Sorry," Andy said and reaching into his pocket peeled off three dollars and gave it to Jake. "Best I can do, Jake."

"But Andy . . ." Jake started, but stopped when Rick came out. "See you in a couple of hours, Rick," said Andy.

"Thanks. I've left all the clothes in the dressing room," said Rick.

They came out and walked silently for a few minutes.

"Listen, Rick, when you go back . . ."

"I know, I know. You want me to get sucked by that damn queer," said Rick, interrupting Jake.

"We are all queers, baby. We are all faggots," said Jake with a hurt note in his voice.

"I hate queers who look so openly like queers," said Rick.

"Listen, Rick, let's not get into a fight. I live by selling myself to queers. So I don't like knocking them. Just listen, okay? We need those clothes. So just be nice to him when you go to see him. Let him be your first customer, okay?" said Jake.

Rick did not reply. They took the subway and got back to their usual haunt, Times Square.

"Where do we go now?" asked Rick as they came out of the subway.

"Nowhere. Let's just hang around, get a cup of coffee, then you can go get the slacks and stuff, dress up and get ready for the big kill tonight," said Jake and hit Rick on the arm to restore the camaraderie that had been lost with the argument over using the word queer.

"You know, come to think of it, it's all pretty sordid," said Rick.

"In this game you shouldn't think. Just hustle, make some dough and quit while you're young," said Jake.

Rick was silent.

"Oh, come on, baby, snap out of it. It's not so bad. Better than beating people over the head and stealing. We work, boy, we work for our living," said Jake.

"I think I'll go sit in some air-conditioned movie for a couple of hours, then go up to Andy's, okay?" asked Rick.

"You and your damn movies. Okay. But, listen, meet me in our office at eight sharp," said Jake.

"Our office?"

"The cafeteria."

"Oh! Okay."

Rick walked on, parting from Jake not so much to see a movie, but to be alone. He wondered if he were doing the right thing. What was his ambition? What was he really doing? But then he needed something to live on, and also needed someone who could befriend him. Anyway he'd try out for a few days. Hell, what's the use of thinking anyway! Jake was right, in this business you must not think. He saw the marquee in front of him advertising the show inside, *The Reluctant Debutante,* starring his favorite actor John Saxon. He went to the box office to buy a ticket.

After the movies he went over to Andy's to pick up the clothes.

The shop was closed, but Andy was waiting impatiently outside.

"Sorry, I'm late," said Rick.

"Let's go," said Andy.

"Where to?"

"To my place, honey. It's just around the corner. Don't look so scared; that's where I do all my tailoring, come on," said Andy.

They walked, and as Andy had said, he did live around the corner in an apartment hotel. They took the elevator to the fifth floor. It was a moderate sized apartment, a large living room, a kitchen, another partition that could be used for either a dressing room or just to keep things, and of course a nice bathroom.

"How do you like it?" Andy asked, closing the door behind him.

"Nice, very nice. You should see the dump where Jake and I stay," said Rick.

"You didn't believe me, did you?" said Andy. He went into the dressing room, came out with a portable sewing machine. "See, I'll fix your cuffs. I don't do this for everybody, you know. They buy things from me and take it somewhere else to get it fixed. This service is only for special people."

"I appreciate it," said Rick.

"Take your things off, honey, relax, make yourself comfy," said Andy as he opened the sewing machine and took out Rick's slacks from the paper bag he had brought with him.

"I'm okay, Andy," said Rick, leaning back on the sofa.

"Suit yourself," said Andy.

After a few minutes, Rick said, "Hey, Andy, is it okay if I take a shower. I feel so sweaty, so sticky."

"Of course, honey. Feel free. I'll get you a fresh new towel and some special soap," said Andy. He got up and went into the bathroom.

"Thanks," said Rick.

"I'll just sit on this toilet seat and watch you," said Andy as Rick took off his T-shirt.

"Oh, Andy. Go get those slacks finished."

"What if you complete your shower by then?"

"I won't. Go on," said Rick, unzipping and chasing Andy out.

"Cock teaser," said Andy and went out.

The full blast of the cold shower felt good, and Rick luxuriated in the rich soapy lather, cleansing his body, and prancing like a young stallion. He could not resist playing with his cock which started to stiffen. When he opened his eyes, and turned off the shower, he saw Andy sitting in front of him.

"Hand me that towel," said Rick.

"Let me dry you, okay?" Andy offered.

"No. Just give me the towel, dammit," said Rick angrily. He pulled the towel away from Andy and dried himself and stepped out of the shower wrapping it around his waist.

"What a body you got, stud. God, what a gorgeous body, and what a juicy piece of meat," Andy kept salivating as they left the bathroom.

"You like my body?" Rick asked.

"Oh, baby, I'm crazy for it."

"Have you seen anyone more gorgeous than myself?"

"None. I've seen studs, baby, lots of them, but you are the very best. I'm crazy for you. I'm your slave, honey. Your obedient slave," said Andy.

Rick stopped in the middle of the living room and stared at Andy and then tantalizingly did a slow strip and dropped his towel. His cock was fully erect, thrust upward. Rick stroked and caressed the shaft, and with his hands on his slim hips he wet his lips with his tongue. Andy drooled.

"Don't just stand there, slave. Suck me. Swallow my cream. Every drop of it," Rick commanded.

Andy fell to his knees and grabbed Rick's muscular thighs and opened his hungry mouth.

It was nearing nine-thirty when Rick came rushing into the cafeteria on Times Square. He had not meant to stay so late with Andy, but the shower, the cool room, and the steamy sex with Andy had all contributed to Rick taking a nice nap. He had awakened with a start, taken another shower, dressed in his new outfit and rushed out, telling Andy that he'd come back for his old clothes. Andy had promised to have them washed and pressed by the time he returned.

Rick felt cocky and confident when he saw heads turned in his direction. He was a stunning young stud in his new clothes. But Rick looked for Jake. He was not there in the cafeteria, and Rick searched for him outside on the street, and finally around ten-fifteen saw Jake in front of a hot dog stand.

"I'm real sorry I'm late. You know what...," Rick started, but was interrupted.

"Never mind, keep walking," said Jake.

They kept walking on Broadway and turned into Forty Third Street and stopped where it was slightly dark.

"Listen, let's get a few bucks before we turn in. It's been a damn dirty, sonofabitch evening. Not a single score. One guy says, after talking to me for half an hour and making me walk all the way up to Fifth Avenue, that he'll give me one lousy buck if I shack up with him. I could have bashed that guy, dirty no good fucking sonofabitch," said Jake, furiously pounding his fist into his palm. He was all worked up. "And besides, these coppers. Too many of them tonight," he added.

"Maybe we should just close up tonight," suggested Rick.

"Close up? Listen, kid, we ain't got a nickel. So you better go out and hustle your sweet tight ass. Let's not talk about going to see some damn movies. I got you those threads you're wearing, and you look rested too. Okay?" Jake exploded.

"Don't push me, Jake. I'm your meal ticket, don't forget that. I can go live with Andy. He'll cater to me. He's my slave. Don't

34

order me around," said Rick in a very calm voice and started to walk away.

Jake came after him. "Sorry, Rick. I'm real sorry for bursting out like that. Apologies. Okay?" he said and put his arm around Rick. "It's just that this evening has been so . . ."

"Forget it. We're both a bit tense. Remember I'm new to this game," said Rick in a conciliatory manner.

"I understand, baby. I understand. Sorry, okay?"

"Okay," said Rick.

They came back to Broadway. They walked on watching the crowds. The plays were over and the people were pouring onto Broadway.

"Let's stop here, for a second," said Jake, pausing near a drug store on the corner of the Sheraton Astor Hotel. As people passed, several looked at them, many longingly at Rick. One or two hovered, hoping to talk to Rick, but Jake again said, "Let's go," and Rick obeyed.

"There were quite a few potential cocksuckers," Rick said.

"Yeah, I know. Listen," said Jake as they were walking. "There's a guy in a blue suit, slightly bald, following us, don't look. I'll turn at the next corner and go, you stop a little further down, pretend you're window shopping. He'll come and talk. Don't go for less than twenty-five. Start with thirty or even thirty-five. Keep casually stroking your crotch, say how big it is. Say you're a college student from California, that you were visiting here, lost your wallet, that you've never done this before, but have to. Okay? Tell him that story. He's a regular cruiser. I've seen him before, drives a stylish Thunderbird. So he's got the dough. In fact I'd even ask for fifty. Why not? Yeah, ask him for fifty. You deserve that price. Good luck."

"But, Jake . . ."

"Don't be nervous, kid. You'll make out fine. I'll be around to help you if there should be any trouble," said Jake, and slinked away on the next street.

Rick walked on, stopped in front of a record shop, and started looking at the window display. As though it had been a pre-arranged drama, a man came up and started looking at the window, too. It was the slightly balding man in the blue suit, middle aged, trim, broad shouldered. He reminded Rick of Mr. Helms, his high school football coach. They both stared at the window display for some time, and Rick got a bit impatient. He looked up at the man, and the guy smiled rather sheepishly.

Hesitantly, yet wanting to get it over with, Rick looking in front of him and avoiding the man's face asked, "Looking for fun?"

"Yes," the man said very gently.

His gentle voice gave courage to Rick.

"Do you like me?"

"Sure. You are possibly the most attractive boy I've ever seen here," the man said.

Rick noticed that a few others had gathered around, hovering, waiting to move in if the transaction failed, so that they could trade for Rick's meat.

Rick became a bit self-conscious with the gathering of prospective buyers around him. So he said, "Buy me some coffee, then we can talk."

"With pleasure," the man said and they walked on.

They went to a restaurant nearby and sat in a booth, and ordered coffee. Rick noticed that the man was rather shy and well mannered.

"Where are you from?" Rick asked.

"Billings, Montana."

"Come all that way?"

"Yes. I have business here, so I come here frequently. This time I had to be in Jacksonville, Florida with my family. I left them there and took a flight out to New York. I have to get back tomorrow. I'll be back next month for a few days," he explained.

"With your family? You married?" Rick asked, surprised.

"Strange, isn't it?" the man asked and, taking out a wallet, showed a picture of his family, his wife and himself with three children, a boy and two girls.

"What do you know? I wouldn't have believed it," said Rick.

The man smiled sheepishly again and put his wallet back.

"And you like boys?" Rick asked.

"Yes."

"You come all this way to get a boy?"

"Billings is a small place. I have to be careful. New York gives me anonymity. Besides, where would I find someone so attractive as you?" the man said.

"I'm expensive," said Rick.

"I would be disappointed if you weren't."

"You see, I don't do this for a living. I'm training to be an actor," said Rick.

"Sure. You don't look like some common hustler," the man said.

36

The compliment pleased Rick.

"You also remind me of my highschool football coach." said Rick.

"Did you have a secret crush on your coach?" the man asked with a smile.

"Now that you ask, I guess I did."

"Then you'll have a good time with me."

"I'll give you the best time you've ever had."

"I'm so glad I met you."

"I am too. It'll cost you fifty bucks," said Rick.

"That's a lot."

"I got a lot of meat too," said Rick.

The man smiled and took out his wallet to pay for the coffee.

"Fifty? Agreed?" Rick asked and stood up, artfully adjusting his bulge to rest on the table.

The man nodded.

They left.

6

RICK BECAME A CONSUMMATE PROFESSIONAL hustler. The signs, the gestures, the secretive eye movements of the secret homosexual world among the subways around Times Square became familiar to him. He was able to size up potential customers, make the needed contacts, effectively negotiate his terms, and satisfy the hungry erotic desires of his clients. He became adept at quickie jobs and equally expert at long all night affairs. He liked it best when men drooled over him, crooning how handsome he was, how virile he was, what a horsy cock he had, and grew ecstatic over his staying power. He tantalised his clients, making sure he took the money first before he upzipped.

Jake wanted Rick to hustle during the days also, but Rick kept his working hours, as he called it, between ten at night to around three in the morning. He saw movies other times, or sat in cafeterias reading movie magazines and arrogantly dismissing guys who sought his favors.

But they still stayed in the same dump, and whenever Rick mentioned the idea to move to a better place, Jake always asked him to wait a little longer, for the money was getting bigger and soon they would be able to hit the sunny areas of Florida or California. By the time Rick got back, Jake would be asleep or out; and by the time Rick got up around noon or later, Jake would be out. So they met rarely. Once in a while they used to have breakfast together, or meet when Rick got home early in the morning. If Rick was in the mood he would tell Jake about his experiences; if not he would just go to sleep. Once or twice Jake had tried to make love to Rick, but Rick had cut him short. After that first night they had met, they had not had sex together again.

But Jake always collected the money, which he was supposed to deposit in Rick's account, for Rick had opened a deposit account a few days after he started hustling.

It had been Labor Day weekend, and Rick's body had been enjoyed by quite a few who had come to the big city seeking fun and laughter. He was tired when he woke up after the long weekend and he felt hot and sticky. Jake was out, and Rick decided that he was definitely going to move out of that dump where he was sleeping. He was going to have it out with Jake that day, he decided. He got up, dressed and came out.

He had breakfast, and when he came out the sun was fierce. His T-shirt and his thin white cotton trousers stuck to his body. He got a hair cut, and decided to go see Andy, whom he had not seen since that day he bought the slacks and shirt he was wearing.

"Am I dreaming or is it true? I can't believe it," said Andy, looking at Rick.

"Hello Andy."

"Rick, Rick, where have you been? I looked all over for you, waited for hours near Times Square. Gosh it's good to see you. You look a little tired. Working hard?" Andy asked with genuine concern.

"Sort of."

"How's Jake?"

"Okay, I guess."

"Why? Haven't you seen him. By the way, where do you guys stay?"

"Same dump."

"Same dump. You must be kidding. Listen, honey, with what you got, you must be piling up money," going to the front of the store, and putting up a "Store Closed for the Day" sign.

"You closing? Where you going?"

"Nowhere honey. I just want to talk to you. Want no one to disturb us. Then I want to take you home, where you can take a shower, and rest. I'll give you a nice massage, cook you a nice dinner and give you a fantastic kneetrembler blowjob. How does that sound?" Andy asked and cupped Rick's crotch.

"I don't care what Jake says, I'm going to move out of that dump," Rick said and removed Andy's palm from his crotch.

"Good for you. Where are you moving to?"

"Some place where there's a decent shower. God, how I'd love to swim and swim and swim, forever," Rick said with nostalgia.

"Listen, baby, why don't you move in with me. Just listen before you say yes or no. I got a nice place. Do as you like, come when you want, go when you want, but stay with me. I'll give you an extra key. I'll take real good care of you. You'll brighten my life, make me young again. You can even help me with my store. With you around, it'll attract a larger clientele. All the queens will pour in. What do you say?"

"I don't know."

"Think, honey, think."

"I will. Listen, can I come up and relax in a hot bath?"

"By all means, baby, by all means."

After Rick had had his bath, which Andy had observed intently, Rick said, "Seriously, you know some place, not too expensive I can move into?"

"Seriously you ought to move into this place," said Andy taking the towel and drying Rick.

"No, Andy, it won't work. I want to be on my own," Rick said.

"You will be on your own here. I promise. Alright, I have another idea. Why don't you move into another apartment right here in this hotel? A studio apartment, and you can always use my place for anything you want. I really want to be close to you, sweetie," Andy pleaded.

"That's a good idea," said Rick, dressed by now.

"You should have left those clothes for me to have cleaned and pressed for you. I could have given you a new pair of jeans," Andy said.

"You are sweet, Andy. You know that," Rick said and kissed Andy on the cheek.

Andy was overwhelmed with this affection.

"I'll come back later, okay?" Rick said heading for the door.

"Please do. I'll have a great dinner ready for you. I'm a very good cook, you know," Andy said.

"Sounds terrific," said Rick and left.

He went over to the bank, but was shocked to find that there was only twenty-eight dollars in his account, the first deposit he had ever made. In fury he went back to his room and waited for Jake.

Jake returned around four in the afternoon, haggard and weary.

"Hey, how are you, stranger? Haven't seen you in ages," said Jake, kicking his shoes off and sitting on the bed.

Rick, who was sleeping on the bed, moved a little further down towards the wall.

"You look nice," said Jake, trying to caress Rick's thigh.

"Cut it out, willya," Rick screamed.

"Don't be sore at me, baby. It's been a rough few days."

"Listen, Jake. What have you done with all my money?" asked Rick leaping out of the bed.

"I've put it in the bank. In your account, like I told you. The bundle's getting bigger. Just a few more weeks then we hit sunny Florida, lie on the beach. I know this rich guy in the . . ."

"Oh, shut up. Just shut your trap. You know you haven't put my money in the bank," Rick interrupted. Jake tried to speak, but Rick stopped him by saying, "Don't lie again, Jake, don't. Oh, God, how foolish could I have been to trust you with all my money? Well, give it to me, what's left of it. I'm getting the hell out of here. Give it to me," Rick demanded. He put on his shoes and started throwing his few items into his gym bag.

"Listen, Rick. Please don't get mad at me," Jake said and got up. He put his arm around Rick and tried to hug him. Rick pulled away in anger.

"Don't touch me. Where's my money?"

Jake did not answer, but slumped back on the bed.

"I'm asking you, where's all my money?" Jake did not answer. So now Rick began to shake him, crying out, "Come on, where's my money. Where?"

"It's gone, gone, baby, gone, but I'm going to make it up to you. I sure will. I promise. But please don't leave me baby, don't. I love you. I really do. I'd die if you left me, Rick. Honest," cried Jake.

"Money gone? Gone where?"

"But I'm going to kick the habit, baby, sure kick it. I sure will," said Jake, looking imploringly at Rick.

"You mean drugs?"

"Yeah, but it's a promise, no more . . ." moaned Jake.

"Goddamn, you sonofabitch," said Rick, slamming the door in Jake's face. He ran down the stairs, out of the hotel and onto the street.

He stopped for a few minutes. He shook his head violently, trying not to think about what happened, and walked on hurriedly to Andy's place.

"Hey, you *did* keep your promise," said Andy, beaming with joy, opening the door and letting Rick in.

"I've left Jake," said Rick, matter-of-factly.

"Come stay with me, honey, the place is yours."

"Yeah, I will . . ."

"You agree?"

"Sure. Don't you want me?"

"Honey, honey, I'm the happiest man on earth," Andy said. His eyes grew misty. He tried to hug Rick, but Rick quietly stepped back.

"Listen, Andy, there's one thing we gotta get straight. That is, I go when I like, come when I want. You don't own me. Understand. I know that I gotta let you suck my dick. I know that I gotta fuck you. That I'll do. But no ownership," said Rick.

"Agreed, honey, agreed. Oh, I'm so happy, so happy," said Andy.

7

R ICK RELAXED AFTER MOVING in with Andy. He stopped hustling. Andy gave him clothes, took him out to dinner when he
didn't feel like fixing anything at the apartment. Rick hung around
the apartment, getting up when he pleased, going to the movies, and
not bothering about working or making money. He would go with
Andy often to the store, and there was no doubt that in good stylish
clothes he was quite a draw. Andy's shop soon began to hum with
business from the gay community.

Now that he had time, Rick gave himself over to primping more
carefully. He would soak in the big bathtub luxuriously filled with
many fragrances that Andy had collected. He would look lovingly
and longingly at his smooth sculptured nude body in the mirror. He
had put on the right amount of weight so that his buttocks were
round and his thighs muscular and his chest filled out. He fell in love
with his own reflection in the mirror. This self-discovery of his body
gave him self-confidence and with it came cocky arrogance, and
enormous self-indulgence. He also showed contempt and scorn for
those who hungered after him.

Realizing the extraordinary beauty of his body, Rick began to take
good care of it, and although the sun was now scarce, he tried to get
as much of it as possible on the open terrace above the apartment.
Andy, who was bewitched by Rick's overpowering beauty and virility, catered to every need and pleasure with the devout obedience of
a slave.

But Rick secretly wanted to leave Andy, make the right contact
and move in with someone richer and more influential. He discarded
his old haunts around Times Square, and looked upon the tight
jeaned, tattooed and tired male hustlers in that area as trash. By
subtly questioning Andy, Rick soon came to know all the gay haunts

of New York, particularly discreet places where the select and wealthy gathered. He dressed well, and his macho good looks soon found him three male lovers. They were all well-to-do and held important corporate positions in New York's financial world. Two were in their thirties, the third in his fifties. None knew of the others' existence, yet they all liked and enjoyed the quiet, satisfactory way in which Rick satisfied their deep yearnings. He had given each of them a phone number of a phone booth in a midtown Manhattan drug store. Every Thursday evening he would wait there for a few minutes, and when the phone rang he would pick it up, and the conversation would be precise:

"Rick?"

"Yes?"

"You okay, dear boy?"

"Splendid."

"Can I see you . . .?" the time and place would be mentioned.

Rick would be prompt in his appointments, dressed like a college kid, in clean levis and crewneck cashmere and button-down Oxford shirt, smelling pleasantly. None of the men asked him probing questions, or asked him to move in with them. Rick liked the arrangement. It was cool, precise and very profitable.

Everything seemed to be going well. Rick saved his money from the three lovers. Andy took care of all his expenses, and life was both relaxed and comfortable until he met Bruce.

Bruce was butch. He used to come to Andy's store occasionally. But after Rick's presence in the store, Bruce came more often. Rick did not pay any attention to him, for after Rick had fallen in love with his own body, he had developed a sense of keen pleasure in being particularly indifferent towards those who he knew were hot for his gorgeous body.

But Bruce seemed equally determined to conquer Rick. And rebuffs from Rick only seemed to increase his determination to have sex with Rick. One afternoon when Andy was in the apartment, Bruce found Rick alone in the store, and started a conversation as usual.

"Pardon my curiosity, but how come a stunning well hung stud like you has ended up in a dumpy store like this?" Bruce asked.

"It's none of your damn business. What do you want to buy? Just get it and beat it," said Rick.

"Wow, you do insult customers, don't you?" said Bruce smiling.

Rick did not reply.

Bruce started looking at some slacks.

"May I try this on?" he asked, taking an olive colored pair of slacks.

"Go ahead," said Rick indifferently.

Bruce disappeared into the dressing room, came back with the slacks on, turned in front of Rick and asked, "You think it's okay?"

"It's okay."

"Oh, come on. Put a little more pep in your approval. Show some enthusiasm," said Bruce. "I'm going to a special party. Tony's party, not just any party. I've got to look just right," Bruce said.

"Who's Tony?"

"I don't believe you asked that question," said Bruce in a shocked tone.

"What is he, God's gift to mankind?"

"Tony's the wealthiest gay in town. He's throwing the biggest gay party ever. And believe you me, when he throws a bash, the most famous producers, directors, actors are there. Every stud wants to go to his party, but only the lucky ones get invited. It's at Tony's party that the miracle and magic happens," Bruce said breathlessly.

"What miracle? What magic?" Rick asked.

"The miracle of being discovered. The magic of becoming a movie star," Bruce said and stripped to his black bikini, and tossed the olive slacks on to a chair.

"You want these slacks?" Rick asked picking them up.

Easing into his levis, Bruce said, "Not snug enough. I think I'll find a better pair at Bloomingdale's."

"What is this movie star bit you mentioned?" Rick asked, his curiosity obviously sharpened.

"You *are* from hicksville, aren't you?" asked Bruce. "The party, that's where a guy gets noticed by some big-shot director or pro-ducer or movie star. If that happens, that's the miracle, the magic. The lucky stud flies to Los Angeles, or Rome or wherever, and becomes a star. See you," Bruce said in a very smug manner and left.

Rick sat thinking for a few minutes. If what Bruce said was true, then this was his big chance. This was precisely what he wanted, to be discovered and turned into a star. He got up, walked over to the mirror in the dressing room and looked at himself. I'm handsome, he said to himself. He turned around and caught his reflection from several angles and felt deliriously happy at his beauty. He caressed his buns, stroked his thick shaft till it started to stiffen. All I need is for

45

the right person to see me, he thought. No, he couldn't afford to let Tony's party pass him by. But how to get invited. Best thing was to talk to Bruce. If it meant getting sucked by Bruce, well, he'd do it. Bruce was a good looking stud, too. In fact, he was turned on by him, Rick admitted to himself. He rummaged through Andy's drawers to see if there was a phone number listed for Bruce. Andy had a book of phone numbers, but Bruce wasn't there.

He closed the store and went back to the apartment. Andy was wrapped around in a thin red dressing gown, working at the sewing machine.

"Hi, Rick. Back so soon? I'm glad you are, was feeling lonesome. How did it go? Any business?" Andy asked as Rick slumped on the couch.

"Andy, do you know anything about Tony's party?" Rick asked.

"You mean the interior decorator?"

"I think so. Bruce mentioned him. Told me that Tony was giving a big party and all the top producers and movie stars would be there," said Rick, removing his clothes.

"I've never been to one, honey. It's supposed to be very very elite. I hear he throws big affairs," said Andy.

"I'd like to go. You know how I can go?" Rick asked, stripping down to his skin tight red shorts.

"That looks good on you. Very sexy. But then anything'll look good on you," Andy said.

"Yes, I know," said Rick examining himself. "You know where Bruce lives?"

"No. But I know he hangs around a bar in the Village."

"Which bar?"

"It's called Ganymede."

"I think I'll go look for him," said Rick.

"I wouldn't recommend the party, Rick. It might get wild, drugs all that kind of stuff."

"I don't mind. I got introduced to the wildness of the city the moment I got here, in the basement of a moviehouse," said Rick.

Andy remained silent.

"I think I'll take a nice shower before I go looking for Bruce," said Rick, going to the bathroom.

"Rick," said Andy and followed him. "Take it from an old pro. Don't go to any parties."

"What did you say?" shouted Rick over the sound of the shower.

"I wouldn't go if I were you."

"You can't even if you want to. Who'd invite an old guy like you?" said Rick, coming out of the shower. "Look at yourself in that mirror. All that fat belly flesh. It's disgusting. Why don't you take care of yourself, stay slim and young. Look at my body, isn't it gorgeous," said Rick stepping out of the shower dripping wet.

"You can't always be young, Rick," said Andy giving him a fresh big towel.

"I'll always be young," said Rick drying himself.

"Get me a new bikini, the white one with the blue side stripe," Rick ordered.

Andy walked back to the bedroom and went through the drawer to get what Rick wanted.

Rick eased into it, adjusted his balls and cock to arouse Andy, splashed cologne on his body, carefully combed and brushed his hair. Then he selected a blue and white striped shirt, and a pair of white linen slacks. "Don't I look smashing?" he asked Andy and said, "Get me a sandwich, chicken, white meat."

"Fix it yourself," said Andy.

"Fix it myself? Go fix it, you faggot slave. Get off the fat jello can of yours. Come on, up," said Rick with contempt.

"What's gotten into you today? You act like a bitch," said Andy, his lips trembling with anger and disappointment.

"Don't call me a bitch, you fat old auntie of a queer," said Rick.

"You call *me* a queer! Who the hell do you think *you* are?" screamed Andy.

Rick did not reply but stepped into his moccasins, put a red scarf around his neck, and took a car coat in his hand.

"Where you goin?" Andy asked in a softer voice.

"Some damn place where I can get a bite to eat."

"Rick, forget it. I'm sorry. I think we both said a lot of things in a weak mood. Give me just five minutes. I'll dress up. Then I'll take you to a very nice restaurant and we'll have a quiet dinner, and then go see a movie. Okay?" Andy said reaching out to touch Rick.

"Don't touch me," Rick shouted, and dashed out, slamming the door.

Rick went to a drug store, ordered a hamburger and a glass of milk. Then he went to the Village to see if he could find Bruce, for above all else he was now obsessed with the desire to get to this party. He even visualized his entrance, the immediate turning eyes in his direction. For after all, wasn't he a good-looking stud, robust, vigorous and hung like a young stallion? He felt more conscious than ever before of the thrust of power and vitality in his crotch. Yes, he would make a hit at that party, be picked up by some big director, and bingo—after a hot session in bed—Rick would emerge a star. But the important thing was to get to the party, and at the moment it looked as though Bruce was his only contact towards realizing that aim.

He walked all around the Village, peering into restaurants and bars, and getting a charge out of people staring at him. Then he walked into Ganymede.

Ganymede was a bar attached to a restaurant, very chic, very plush. All Rick had with him was about three dollars, but that did not bother him. His face was his money, his body was his money, his super cock was his fortune. He looked in the bar, surveying the elegantly dressed young men to see if Bruce was there. Then he walked into the restaurant, took off his car coat, and the scarf, and sat in a small, wood-paneled booth. He ordered an espresso.

"Just an espresso?" the waiter asked.

"What else do you suggest?"

"The minimum charge is two dollars."

"Go get me the espresso, I have a rich sugar daddy," Rick said with contempt.

He leaned back and saw quite a few who were at the bar leave their seats to wander close to his seat, to sniff around. He was fresh meat, and they all wanted him. To Rick, who was now quite familiar with the subtle movements of the male pursuing the male, the migration around his table in the restaurant by these young men and not-so-young men meant that he was the stud. He felt supremely satisfied. Follow me, follow me, come see my big juicy cock, see my butch buns, drool over my meat, he said to himself with a smile on his lips as he got up and walked to the wash room, a red-carpeted, fragrant-smelling place. He was proved correct in his predictions for quite a few followed him. Rick stood in front of the mirror, brushed back his dark wind-blown hair, washed his hands, and moved to the urinals. Two guys moved on either side of Rick. Rick unzipped slowly and took his time taking out his cock and slowly shook it and it stiffened. He made certain that the two guys saw his meat, then he stuffed it back in the pouch of his bikini and zipped up. The bulge was bursting. One of the guys followed Rick out and asked Rick for a match. Cockily Rick replied, "Buy one," and walked on.

He sat and sipped his coffee, feeling good that he had teased and aroused these men. Then suddenly a thought came to him, and the very thought of what he'd do to Andy gave him a hardon.

He put down two dollars and walked out of Ganymede, without finishing his espresso. He looked in a few more bars, but not finding Bruce, he took the subway and returned to the apartment. He undressed quietly, and went to the bathroom, locked it from within and turned on the shower full blast.

"Is it you, Rick, have you come back?" he heard the shouting of Andy, and his knocking on the door.

Rick stopped the shower, rubbed himself dry, slowly played with his cock till it started to lengthen and stiffen, gently wrapped the towel around his waist, tousled his dark hair so that it fell over his forehead giving him a seductive look, and came out.

"Oh, Rick, I'm glad, so glad you returned," Andy cried out, his eyes filled with tears as he followed Rick, trying to touch him.

"Keep your hands off!" Rick screamed. "I'm here only to pack and leave."

"Leave? What do you mean?" Andy asked, his voice quivering with anxiety.

Rick went to the bedroom and came out with his old gym bag. "I'm not taking a single item belonging to you. Where's my old torn and tattered levis?" he asked.

"Rick, please. Honey, baby, sweetheart, listen to me. Please sit down. Please," Andy begged.

"Don't touch me," Rick said.

"Agreed. I won't touch you. But please listen to me. Please."

"Where's my levis?" Rick asked looking around and giving Andy tantalizing glimpses of his stiff erection.

"I'll do whatever you want, Rick."

"Whatever I want?"

"Yes."

"You'll be my obedient slave?"

"I am your slave."

"You'll kiss my feet?"

Andy knelt and kissed Rick's feet.

"Say you're a dog."

"I'm a dog."

"Are you hungry for me?"

"Oh, Rick, am I ever!"

"Let your tongue hang out."

Andy obeyed.

Rick turned and dropped his towel and spread his legs. "Lick my

49

ass hole," he ordered.

Andy gripped Rick's thighs and started to ream him.

"Deeper, deeper, you bastard. Eat out my ass," Rick ordered.

Andy increased his intensity.

Rick moaned with joy. Then he quickly turned and stood up. The sight of his stiff erection excited Andy. A pearly drop of cum glistened on Rick's large velvety knob.

"Lick that drop," Rick ordered.

Andy leaned forward and obeyed.

Rick clasped Andy by his hair and said, "You are my slave?"

Andy nodded.

"Suck my meat, you dog. Suck it all the way. Clean my pipe. Suck, you bastard, suck," Rick ordered.

Andy drooled and opened his mouth for Rick's trembling meat.

8

B RUCE BUILT UP GREAT ANTICIPATION in Rick about Tony's party. He described in great detail those who were likely to come, what their special sexual desires were, how they would dress, and what their professions were. He elaborated on the fact that Tony's party would be the meeting place of Hollywood producers, directors, film stars, and playwrights. Tantalizingly, Bruce spun stories of young men who managed to get to Tony's parties and get spotted by the right people. Now they were acting as escorts to rich old men, houseboys to movie stars, frolicking in the world's playgrounds, driving swanky cars, wearing elegant clothes, and dining out in the most exclusive restaurants. Bruce was very persuasive and he soon had Rick drooling over his stories, hoping for the miracle to happen. Bruce had hungered for Rick's pliant and gorgeous body, and Rick eagerly satisfied every one of Bruce's strange and often kinky sexual tastes. Rick had considered himself the dominant male in all his relationships, but now with Bruce he passively turned over to let Bruce fuck him uninhibitedly. At the same time, Rick began to enjoy sex with Bruce. The hard athletic body of Bruce, the strength and virility of Bruce, turned him on, and Rick sucked Bruce's throbbing cock with unconcealed passion and desire.

Rick became a stranger to Andy's apartment. He would be away for days, together with Bruce. He stopped hustling and began to spend what money he had saved to keep Bruce happy, for Rick was now completely obsessed with the desire of getting to Tony's party. He even managed to give Bruce clothes from the store, without charging him. Bruce took Rick out to interesting spots, where Rick spent the money he had earned from his three rich lovers. Being young, hung and handsome, Rick naturally attracted attention at these chic spots, and felt desired by every man who glanced his way.

Meanwhile, Andy sank deeper and deeper into melancholy. He yearned for Rick, longed for his body, and went looking for him, but both Rick and Bruce had discreetly kept their address secret. Once in a while Rick would get to the apartment, and find Andy, but he would rush back after a quick "hello" or "good evening." It was at these times that Andy's desires reached a fever pitch, for Rick would give him glimpses of his naked body, of his splendid cock. After Rick had left, Andy would go out cruising and pick up some tight-trousered hustler to satisfy his passion, imagining all the while it was Rick's body he was loving.

But Andy was unable to find the fire and charged male sexuality from these hustlers that generated from Rick. He wondered why he had fallen prey to such an obsessive attachment. Andy had never tried to build a lasting friendship with any boy. He had sought his pleasure purely on a business level, finding accommodating young men for a night or two by paying money. After it was over, it was over. Nothing was left behind. But with Rick, it had been different. Rick had gotten inside his skin, and however hard Andy tried, he was unable to shake off his special longing for this handsome, young, arrogant boy with the gorgeous body.

As the weeks passed, Tony's party did not seem to come off. Bruce kept saying that it was postponed because some big shot was unable to come, a big producer who was going to be the guest of honor. Money was running out, and Rick was getting more anxious.

Bruce had stayed out all night once, and got in to the apartment around ten the next morning.

"Where were you?" asked Rick.

"It's a big story, Rick, a big story. But I think you're in luck," said Bruce, as he stripped.

"You mean the party?"

"Yeah."

"Great, when?" Rick asked excitedly.

"It's better than that, Rick—we're meeting Tony this evening."

"Where?"

"Fix me some breakfast, will you, Rick? I'll tell you all about it as I soak in the tub and eat some breakfast," said Bruce, going to the bathroom.

Rick followed as Bruce turned on the tap, and eased himself into the tub. "Where's the breakfast?" Bruce asked.

"In a minute. I'll fix it. Please tell me. The details," Rick asked.

"You see, last night I was at this party. I'm sorry, Rick. It came so unexpectedly, I mean the invite, that I was unable to get in touch with you. Anyway, I went. And surprise of surprises, Tony was there. We got to talking and I told him about you."

"About me?"

"Of course. I'm always promoting you wherever and whenever I can. You know that!"

"Yes, of course, Bruce. Continue."

"I told him what a stunning looking hunk you were. How superbly hung. Fresh, wholesome, how you love to get fucked . . ."

"Bruce," Rick interrupted. "You're the only one I've allowed to fuck me."

"Don't worry! From what I hear, Tony loves to get mounted," said Bruce.

"Then why did you tell him that I loved to take it up my ass?" Rick questioned.

"Does it make such a big difference! For crying out loud. Are you giving me the third degree? Jesus Christ, here I am promoting you . . ." Bruce angrily splashed his hands in the water.

"I'm sorry, Bruce. I didn't mean to . . ." Rick started to apologize.

"Never mind. I should never have invited Tony to dinner this evening," Bruce interrupted.

"Tony? Dinner? Where?" Rick asked.

"At the Zodiac. Just the three of us, at eight. A few cocktails, then dinner. Tony loves fish and the Zodiac is noted for their seafood. I know Roger, the maitre d', and he'll give us a nice quiet table. Imagine, just us three. Why, it's a dream. You turn on the charm. I know you will make a big hit with him. He'll extend the invitation to his party. I'm dead certain, and you're bound to be the sensation of the season. But . . ."

"But what?" Rick asked.

"The Zodiac is an expensive restaurant. Roger has to be tipped for the table we are getting. Besides we can't quibble about what Tony selects. We must order the right kind of wine. It'll be worth it, Rick. Believe me," said Bruce.

"How much are we talking about?" Rick asked.

"Anywhere from fifty to seventy bucks. Consider it as an investment."

"God, Bruce, I haven't got that kind of money. I can get it in a few days if I hustle . . ."

"No. I don't want you to hustle. You're star material, Rick. You really are. I don't want you dropping your pants for a quick blow job. Go to Andy. Hear me out," said Bruce as he instructed. "Andy's got the hots for you. Am I right?"

"Yes."

"Go to him. Show him a little affection, let him feel your meat. Take it out, play with it. Let him know what he's missing. Then when he's drooling hit him for the seventy five bucks. He'll give it. Tell him you'll be back and he can suck out your cream. That old queer will fork out the money. Okay?" Bruce said.

Rick was silent.

"Rick, I can call the whole thing off if it's so difficult for you to raise the money. After all, it's the one single break you've been waiting for," Bruce said, sliding further down in the bathtub and closing his eyes.

"I sure hope something comes out of this. I'm counting on it. I've used up all my money and even possibly lost my contacts, since I haven't called them in quite some time," said Rick.

"It'll happen, Rick. It'll happen. It'll happen this evening. Go get the money from Andy. Then get yourself a nice trim haircut. I'll tell you what to wear, and we'll go meet Tony," Bruce said with his eyes closed, his body relaxed.

Rick and Bruce remained silent for a while.

"You think you could at least get me a cup of hot coffee?" Bruce asked.

Rick went and fixed some coffee for Bruce and decided that he would go and get the money from Andy. He gave Bruce a mug of hot steaming coffee, put on a jacket and headed for Andy's apartment.

It was not difficult to get the money from Andy. All Rick had to say was that he was real happy to see Andy, allow Andy to feel his bulge, and then promise to come back and stay with him forever. Andy, who was starved for affection, gave Rick the money.

"I see you got the cash. Ah, you charmer," said Bruce when Rick returned.

"Yeah, but I didn't like it. I promised to see him again. Poor Andy, he got so worked up. I feel rotten, to tell you the truth," said Rick.

"To hell with him. The bastard does not even know how to suck cock. One time he left teeth marks on my meat," said Bruce.

Rick did not like the way Bruce abused Andy, but he kept silent. He hoped that he'd be able to make a hit with Tony that evening, then move in with him. He was getting sick and tired of Bruce. Bruce was becoming much too demanding in bed.

54

Rick went out to get a haircut and when he returned he dressed according to Bruce's instructions. He looked smashing. They left for the Zodiac. Just before they entered the restaurant, Bruce took the money from Rick saying, "It'd look better if I paid."

They went in. It was crowded. They waited for nearly an hour or so in the bar, but no sign of Tony. Bruce kept going out frequently to check and returned saying, "I wonder what happened." Rick politely fought off guys trying to pick him up at the bar. Bruce, however, had picked up a big frat house jock type blond hunk who was downing one martini after another. "Might as well go and order dinner. I'm sure Tony will show up," said Bruce and invited the blond to join him and Rick. Rick simmered with anger but controlled himself.

"Aren't you going to introduce me to your good looking buddy?" the blond asked Bruce.

"I'm Norman," the blond said and shook Rick's hand.

Rick noticed the firm round melon buttocks of Norman and visualized himself giving him a tight hard fuck.

As though reading his mind, Norman leaned close to Rick and said, "Let's skip dinner and go someplace where you can fuck the shit out of me."

Rick edged away from the foul breath of Norman.

"Your friend is not sociable," said Norman to Bruce.

Bruce slipped his arm around Norman and said, "Rick, I know you're disappointed. I honestly don't know what happened. The evening hasn't turned out the way you wanted it, although I can't complain, can I?" He looked up at Norman.

"I like your buddy, but I'll settle for you," Norman said.

"Let's go home," Rick said to Bruce.

"Home?" Bruce questioned, drawing close to Norman.

"Hey, listen," Norman said, lowering his voice. "Why don't we try a threesome or what's it called, menage something or the other."

"Bruce, I'm leaving. Okay?" Rick said and left in anger.

He didn't feel like thinking over what had happened, but got the oppressive feeling that Bruce had taken him for a ride. Tonight when Bruce got back, he was going to have a showdown, he thought. To calm himself down he went to a movie.

His mind was not on the picture, and he returned to the apartment. He tossed restlessly in the bed, took a warm shower, and tried to sleep, but he was unable to sleep. He was thinking of going out again, possibly to find a young guy for sex, when the door opened and Bruce came in. It was a little after 2 A.M.

"Waiting up for me? How nice?" said Bruce, kicking his shoes off. He sat on the chair, took off his socks, and said, "What a Greek god, that Norman. But he wasn't worth a shit in bed. Just lay there, passed out. But you'd have loved that ass of his. Rick, I gotta hand it to you, no one can move their body like you can. You . . ."

"Bruce, why did you lie to me?" Rick said.

"What are you talking about?"

"About today and all these days. I don't think there's any such person called Tony who throws fabulous parties. You made it all up, didn't you?" Rick asked.

Bruce did not reply but went on undressing.

"What a damn fool I was to believe you," said Rick. Then he leaped out of bed, caught hold of Bruce, shook him violently and asked him over and over again, "Why, why did you lie to me, why?"

"Stop it, Rick, stop it, you're hurting me," said Bruce, taken aback with surprise.

"I'll kill you, I will," shouted Rick, pushing Bruce down to the floor.

They were on the floor, wrestling, hitting, and soon Bruce pinned Rick down, sitting on him, squeezing his throat. In frantic fear, Rick reached out, seized an alarm clock on a stool nearby and struck Bruce on the forehead. Shrieking, and stopping the blood that had started to come from his forehead, Bruce let go of Rick.

Rick was frightened when he saw that he had wounded Bruce, so he slipped quickly into a pair of slacks and, taking his jacket and shoes, rushed out of the apartment. It was outside the apartment that he managed to put on his shoes, thrusting his socks into his trouser pockets. Damn it, damn it, damn it, he cursed himself. Here he was dreaming of success and luxury, and here he was now poor and miserable as he was on that first day he had met Jake.

It was cold, and the wind was strong. Andy's seemed like the only place he could go. Yes, Andy, the old faithful. He'd be good to him now, thought Rick, and ran towards Andy's hotel apartment.

Andy waited for Rick, waited patiently and with hope, and at midnight reluctantly admitted to himself that Rick was not coming, and that he had been fooled again.

He put on a top coat, and went out. His mind was a blank, but his desires were sharp and aroused. He kept looking at every young male face. Tired, he entered a cafeteria on Forty Second Street. He went and sat in a corner with a cup of coffee.

He surveyed the scene, and saw two guys outside the cafeteria. Their backs were turned towards him, so that he was unable to see their faces, but he could see through the glass that covered the front of the cafeteria that they were young by their stances. They had big broad shoulders, and the shape of their buttocks and thighs beneath their tight black dungarees excited him. He came out of the cafeteria to examine the merchandise.

He was not disappointed. They were both young and tough, a Nordic blond and a Mediterranean brunette. Their shirts were open inspite of the cold and showed off their well formed pecs. Their bulges were like clenched fists beneath their button front dungarees. Precisely what he wanted, someone young, hard and tough who, by one sheer deep penetration, could give him that special pain tinged with pleasure. He walked in front of them. The dark one was his choice. But it was the Nordic blond who smiled at Andy. Andy returned the smile and walked on, stopping in front of a store. The blond came up.

"Got a place where we can warm up?" the fellow asked.

"You come directly to the point," said Andy

"Why waste time? We both know what we want. Besides, we got to get back to the base."

"Base?"

"Yeah, me and my buddy, we're both in the navy."

The very word "navy" gave Andy a hardon. He adored sailors. His first sex had been with a sailor in his hometown, Providence, forty-some-odd years ago. He had even bought Rick a navy outfit, the thirteen button front pants, the blouse, the cap, the whole bit. He wondered what Rick had done with it.

"So what do you say? Got any Scotch up in your place?" the blond asked.

"Sure I have Scotch," Andy said.

"Then let's go. We'll have a party, the three of us."

"Three?"

"Me, my buddy, you," the blond said looking in the direction of his dark haired buddy, who started to slowly walk towards them.

"I don't need two," said Andy. There was a hint of danger, threatening but exciting.

"You've got to take the both of us. We're inseparable. Besides, two for the price of one," the blond said and touched Andy's shoulder.

Andy hesitated, but he was hypnotized by the raging macho virility in both.

The dark one had joined them.

"I'm Wolfgang, he's Salvatore. I'm cut, he's uncut. You should see his cock, a thick Cuban cigar," the blond said.

Before Andy could say anything, Salvatore had hailed a passing cab. They all got in the back seat, with Andy in the center. Andy thought he'd come just by the strong warm pressure of the thighs of these two studs.

"You got a nice pad, yeah, nice and cozy," said Wolfgang as they entered Andy's apartment. He pulled a chair and sat on it, his legs lifted on to each arm. Salvatore slumped on the couch.

"Where's that Scotch?" Wolfgang asked.

"Make it two tall glasses, a little water," Salvatore instructed.

Andy went into the kitchen to fix the drinks. Salvatore got up and fingered the radio and turned on some music. Andy came back with the drinks.

"Aren't you going to join us?" Wolfgang asked.

"Not now. I want to enjoy sex," Andy said.

Wolfgang laughed. Andy took off his top coat and sat on a foot stool.

Wolfgang sipped his drink and caressed his big bulge. Andy looked intently.

Salvatore unbuttoned and Andy saw the red bikini he was wearing.

"Which one do you want to suck first?" Salvatore asked.

"You want this?" Wolfgang asked and stood up and unbuttoned and took out his thick blond cock.

"Go get it, man. It's all yours," Salvatore encouraged.

Andy hesitated, but Wolfgang was caressing his meat which started to harden. The veins stood out. Andy got up, went over and knelt and was about to touch Wolfgang's cock, when he felt a kick on his back. Andy was bowled over. Salvatore stood menacingly over him and started kicking Andy mercilessly saying, "You dirty stinking queer, damn dirty fairy."

Wolfgang drank his Scotch and smashed the glass to pieces. He turned up the volume of the radio. "Okay, Sal. I think he's had enough. Let's go."

Sal stopped, brushed back his hair from his forehead, and wiped his sweat. Andy, who had not uttered a single word during the assault, lay moaning on the ground, blood dripping from his lips and face.

Both guys rummaged through the top coat, then Wolfgang

shoved his big hands in the pockets of Andy's trousers and pulled out a wallet. He hurriedly examined it. It held about thirty-eight dollars. "Sal," he called to his friend, who was now in the kitchen, "I got the loot, come on." Sal came out with two bottles of Scotch, one unopened and the other half empty. "Look what I got," he said, holding up the bottles.

Wolfgang took one of them, playfully hit Sal's crotch, and said, "Keep it hard. We might get another damn queer, before we call it a night."

"I want to take a leak before we go," Sal said.

"Piss on the queer, he might enjoy it," Wolfgang said.

"Good idea," said Salvatore and handed Wolfgang the Scotch bottle. He then stood over Andy, unbuttoned his dungarees, took out his cock and urinated on Andy.

They left without closing the door or turning off the radio.

Andy lay in that state for some time. Then he got up, and slowly dragged himself to the bathroom. He looked at his ghastly, mutilated face in the mirror. He just sat and stared. An uncontrollable depression seemed to drown him. He walked to the kitchen, but could not find any liquor. He looked at the meat knife on the kitchen sink. Taking it, he returned to the bathroom, undressed, turned the hot water on full blast in the bathtub and looked at his ugly, shapeless nudity in the mirror again. His eyes filled with tears. He shut the tap. Then, seated in the bathtub, forcing himself to stay in the scalding water, he gritted his teeth and cut his throat with the knife.

This is how Rick found Andy when he returned to Andy's apartment.

9

A FTER LOOKING AT THE GHASTLY mutilated body that had once touched him so intimately, Rick had rushed out of the apartment to seek lonely isolation in a dark movie house. He tried hard to repress the thought that he was in some way responsible for Andy's tragedy. Now he had a lot to forget, a lot of rethinking to do. He had to start all over again, not in this city, but somewhere else. Too much had happened too soon.

He thought of his mother for the first time in a long time. He must write to her, he thought. But for the present, it was again a question of survival. He came out of the movie house, and it was snowing outside. He hurriedly crossed the street and went to a drug store. It was empty except for a few guys like himself, all eager to make a few bucks before turning in for the night. As soon as anyone walked in, all the eyes turned to check him out in terms of a potential customer. Seeing Rick, one guy said rather loudly, "Lots of fresh meat, man, lots. Tough competition," and when Rick sat next to him and ordered a coffee, he asked, "How's business?"

"Not so good," said Rick.

"You're telling me," the fellow said and offered Rick a cigarette. Rick declined. "You have a place to sleep?" the guy asked.

"No."

"Usually I sell, but tonight I feel like buying. You can stay at my place. I give good blow jobs," the guy said and laughed and patted Rick on his shoulder.

"No, thanks," Rick said. He did not like the atmosphere. He thought he had left these two-bit hustlers when he had moved in with Andy, and made contact with those three rich lovers. He felt depressed at the realization that he was back on the same turf as before.

He left, hoping to pick up someone, get some money, go to the Y, get a room, a hot shower and sleep. He should have taken some money from Bruce, he thought. Tomorrow would be another day. He was still handsome, still had his thick big cock, he'd bounce back. This time he'd be cautious, very cautious, he decided. He walked, huddling in his jacket, close to the shops, hoping to avoid the snow. A Black man stopped him, and Rick agreed to go with him for a quickie for ten dollars. They went to a hotel.

It was one of those hotels like the one in which Rick had stayed with Jake. Rick unzipped and lay on the bed in the dark but warm room. The Black tried to kiss him, but Rick turned his face away, and the Black did not force him. He took out Rick's cock and said, "Bigger than a Nigger's," and started to suck.

When it was over, Rick wiped himself with the edge of the bed sheet, zipped up and said, "Okay, let's have the dough."

The Black reached for his pants and handed three dollars to Rick.

"Three? Come on, you agreed to ten," said Rick.

"Shit, man, no one gives you ten."

"Hey, come on. You agreed to ten."

"Beat it, kid, beat it. I ought to have fucked your sweet ass. One word out of you and I'll fuck you so raw with my black dick, you won't be able to sit up for a month. So count your blessings and scram," the Black said.

Rick left.

Nothing right seemed to happen to him in the following weeks. He waited for long hours by the phone booth where he once got his calls, but nothing happened. He looked tired and shabby and all he could score were three- and five-dollar clients. His one T-shirt and sport shirt reeked with sweat and his dungarees were filthy. He badly needed a haircut, and somehow that body that once had attracted many, now seemed to have lost its charm. Cold and hungry, he hung around hot dog stands and cafeterias, and literally thrust himself at potential customers. Those who picked him up were old men on social security or college kids who had a buck or two and wanted Rick to suck them. Money was tighter than ever.

Rick began to drift, not thinking, not caring.

December brought heavy snow to the city, and for two days before Christmas he was unable to pick up even a single person. Then came the photographer.

It was Christmas Day, and he came out of his dollar-a-day hotel not even knowing what time it was. "Hey, kid, you have to move out," the fellow at the desk said. "You owe me three nights' rent. This is no charity institution."

"Yeah. I'll pay you today," Rick said.

'Go get yourself a job. Wash dishes, do something, a young stud like you," the man advised.

It was snowing hard, and the clock in one of the shops showed three in the afternoon. He went to a washroom in the Port Authority Bus Terminal, and while washing his face noticed that a fellow was looking at him. Rick fervently hoped he'd score wth this guy. He dried his face with the paper towel and stood at a urinal. The man came and stood next to him. Rick started to caress his cock getting a semi hardon for the man's benefit. But the man did not look in Rick's direction. He walked out, and Rick went to a cafeteria to warm himself with a cup of coffee. There were not many in the cafeteria, and Rick, drinking his coffee, looked up and saw the same man he had seen a few minutes ago at the counter. He did not come and sit in front of Rick, but went over to the front of the cafeteria where a young fellow who looked like a Puerto Rican was sitting. Too bad, thought Rick, someone else stole his bread. But the man was looking at him, and then the Puerto Rican kid also turned and looked at him. Rick wondered what was going on, and thought the fellow was a cop, a plainclothesman. He dressed like that anyway, nice top coat, hat, suit, tie. He didn't like his looks anyway, so Rick felt uncomfortable and left the cafeteria. It was cold and snowing. He huddled on the steps leading down to the subway, and again noticed that the man was walking towards him. Was he following him, Rick wondered. He wanted to lose him, so he ran down the stairway and got into a train, not caring where it was going, and just when he was sure he had avoided the man, he saw him get in the car and sit in front of him, open the *New York Times* and start reading. There was no one in that part of the train. Hell, thought Rick and angrily stared at the man. The man felt his stare, lowered the paper and smiled at Rick.

"How come you following me?" Rick asked.

"What?" the man asked, folded his paper and came over and sat next to Rick.

"You cruising me?" Rick asked.

"Sort of."

"Are you or are you not?"

"I am."

"Then why all this cat-and-mouse game. I showed you what I got," said Rick.

"It's big. I know."

"You want me or what?"

"Of course I want you."

"What's it worth?"

"Thirty, forty, maybe even fifty."

"Dollars?"

The man nodded.

"Must be hard work if you want to pay that kind of money."

"The easiest."

"Tell me."

"All you gotta do is stand bareass and pose."

"Pose?"

"For photographs."

"You're going to take my picture?"

"Yes. That's the idea."

"I'm no muscle boy."

"You got muscle between your legs."

"I never pose nude."

"There's always a first."

Rick did not speak.

"What do you say? All you do is come up to my place, pose the way I want you to. About half an hour of work. Then you dress, take the money and leave. I don't know you, you don't know me," said the man softly, persuasively.

It did sound very easy. Rick needed the money, needed it badly. Maybe he could ask for sixty or seventy, that way he could take a bus and go to California. Right now he could use a nice hot shower, a clean bed and some good food.

"Make it seventy, it's a deal," said Rick.

"Seventy!?"

"Yeah, seventy or nothing," said Rick. "I know you'll sell my photos. That's your business and you'll make a lot more than seventy." He said it confidently.

"For that kind of money you gotta do everything I say."

"Everything you say?"

"Like, you know . . . maybe stay a little longer."

"Yeah, for seventy I'll stay."

They got off at the next stop and took another train heading towards the Bronx.

The man's apartment was on the fifth floor, at the very end of the hall, just a large room with a kitchen. The large room contained an old four-poster bed. Everything was bare. The two windows in the room facing the entrance were closed, covered with thick black cloth. The kitchen had one window, but it seemed to be nailed down. It was warm and comfortable when they got in from the biting cold outside. It got very warm once they were inside. "It sure is very hot," said Rick, looking around. He and the man tried to turn the radiator down, but it had got stuck. They tried the window which was also stuck.

"You live here?" Rick asked.

"No. I just rent it from a guy whenever I need to do some photography," the man replied.

"Okay, let's get it over with. What do I do? Strip, I suppose," Rick said removing his jacket.

"Take off your clothes. I'll do the same," the man said starting to undress.

"You want sex with me, it'll be extra," said Rick.

"No, kid. I don't want sex with you," the man said stripping to his blue boxer shorts. "Now, help me with this," the man said, looking under the bed, and Rick bent over, and they both dragged a leather trunk out. The man opened it and Rick saw that it contained his photographic equipment. They took out two folding lamp stands and set them up facing the bed, and when he put on the switch, the bright lights only added to the sultry atmosphere.

"Boy, this makes it hotter," said Rick.

"Take off your clothes and relax," the man said.

Rick stripped and fell on the bed nude, closing his eyes. A few minutes later, he asked with his eyes closed, "What do I do, just sleep like this?"

"Yeah. Take a nap if you want to, until the other kid shows up."

"What other kid?" asked Rick, jumping up from the bed.

"He's from San Juan, Puerto Rico."

"What's he got to do with me?"

"You and he are going to put on a show, and I take the photos."

"Oh, no. That wasn't the deal," said Rick trying to ease into his dungarees.

"Listen, kid, you're not going to run out on me now?"

"What if I do? You going to beat me up?"

"No, kid. That's not my style. You want to leave, you go right ahead. If I'd known, I'd have picked another blond kid who was ready and eager. In fact José, the Puerto Rican, preferred the blond, except that the blond is not hung like you . . ."

64

"No one's hung like me," Rick said angrily.

"You may be right,' the man said smiling.

Rick put on his shirt.

"Before you go, just think. Okay? You won't run into a deal like this where you can pick up good money in a lump this easy. Out there you gotta hustle your butt to pick up a lousy buck or two, and in your present state, that's tough. So . . ." the man shrugged his shoulders.

"Make it eighty," Rick bargained.

"Seventy is what I promised. Seventy is what you'll get. So make up your mind," the man said.

Rick undressed.

"Wise decision," the man said.

"Turn off all these damn lights until that other kid comes. It's too damn hot," Rick said falling on the bed nude.

The man turned off the lights.

About an hour later José arrived, and tried to explain in halting English that he had taken the wrong subway and gotten lost. The man smiled and told him to take off his clothes. Rick noticed that he was the same kid he had earlier seen in the cafeteria. José was probably in his twenties, with thick tight curly dark hair and a tight muscular body. He had a smooth honeybrown complexion. José stripped to his sweaty red jockstrap and smiled sheepishly at Rick. Then he slowly eased down his jockstrap and showed his long uncut cock. Scratching his balls he went over and sat next to Rick.

The man told them the "plot" of the movie. Rick was supposed to be lying on the bed wearing his dungarees. José was to enter with a towel around his waist and kiss Rick. Then Rick gets up, they wrestle playfully with each other and try to remove each other's clothes. They get nude. This was the opening. From then on the man was going to shout the instructions and Rick and José had to obey them.

José said he'd do everything and anything except kiss Rick.

"It's against his macho spirit," the man explained.

"Jesus, he's going to get fucked by me. How's that okay with his macho?" Rick asked.

"Let's not fight, okay," the man calmed Rick.

So they performed. Rick got into the action, feeling good about making love to another hard bodied young guy and he had to admit that José did give him one of the best blow jobs he'd ever had. He was turned on by José's strong musky sweat that covered his body, particularly under his armpits and his crotch. José therefore aroused him to a feverish intensity so that when Rick mounted him, he was not just acting for the camera but enjoying every deep thrust. The whole action lasted for about an hour and a half. After it was over both lay completely exhausted on the bed.

"A great performance kids, just great," praised the man. "You know, I'm strictly a cunt eater, but after I seen you two tango, I got the hots for both of you. See what I mean," the man said pointing to his hard erection thrusting out of his boxer shorts.

"José will take care of you. He gives great head," Rick said.

Rick felt he could sleep forever. He got up to get dressed. His knees buckled under him. He had never known such delirious exhaustion. He saw José sleeping, stretched out in a wild, animal-like pose of utter sensual abandon. Rick struggled and got up.

"Rest a while," the man said. "What's the hurry? Sleep. Then I'll buy you both a Christmas dinner, and then I'll try this new experience with you. You can make a few more bucks."

"No, sorry. Give me the dough, what's coming to me and I'll beat it," said Rick.

"Have it your own way. Guess I gotta take on José," the man said, giving Rick the money. "Here's a little Christmas present," he added another ten.

"You're okay. Yeah, you're okay," said Rick, feeling genuinely appreciative of this man who had kept his deal.

"Maybe we'll run into each other again, if ever I make another movie," said the man.

"My next movie will be in Hollywood," Rick said and hurried out of the room.

Rick headed straight for the Y, got a room, and hardly had he entered it, than he kicked off his shoes, flung himself on the bed, and went to sleep.

10

Rick felt refreshingly relaxed when he woke up after a good long sleep. He took a shower, went out and satisfied his ravenous hunger.

The following morning he bought himself a new pair of tight Levis, a warm fleecelined hooded sweat shirt. He put them on in the store and, coming out into the street, he dumped his dirty old dungarees and T-shirt into a garbage can. He relaxed for the next few days, not hustling, but just eating, sleeping and going to the movies. But the weather was getting colder, money was running out again, and Rick knew that he had to think about what he was going to do next.

For want of some companionship, he began to be a little more communicative with the group of hustlers around Times Square. They met, or hung around a cafeteria on Forty Second Street. There were quite a variety, the tough ones in Levis and leather jackets, showing their tattoo marks with long side burns; the crew cut, muscle-bound guys; the slim, pale, arty types; the studs with tight pants revealing their bulging baskets; lean, wiry Blacks, with hair dyed to blond or red. And late at night would come the queens, heavy with make-up and perfume and mascara. There were the old, fat men, balding, but still trying to dress like young priapic teenagers in tight pants from which protruded their ugly, flabby bellies. And there were also the young and naive ones, hoping to make the big time. Rick met a few clean cut college kids, too, in their crewneck cashmere sweaters and tight chinos, who hustled to make a few fast bucks from "some old queer" whom they beat up after taking his money.

But they all seemed to live on hope, on delusions of grandeur. There was dark, handsome Laredo of Spanish stock, who proudly announced that he rolled queers and was looking for one rich queer someday whom he could roll for the "big" bundle; there was Gatto, who hoped to be discovered in Miami by some wealthy millionaire and sail the high seas in luxury, but Gatto did not even have enough money to get to Florida; there was Dwayne, looking for a rich sugar daddy; and Paris, who wanted to make thirty bucks a day but was not even making five. There were, of course, innumerable young men who hoped to end up as movie stars. Rick would sit and listen to their conversations, their dreams and hopes, and wondered if he too would end up merely dreaming and getting fat and ugly and old and rejected.

He had fallen into just such a melancholy mood on the last day in December. It was late afternoon, soon it would be New Year's Eve. He sat in the cafeteria wondering what he should do. He had tried earlier to make a collect call to his mother, but the operator had said that the number was no longer in service. The thought that his mother might have moved or even died added to his sense of depression. Morning would bring the need to renew his room and the need for money. He missed Andy. He hated to hustle, be pawed over by men, and then tossed a few bucks. But what was the alternative, take a dishwasher's job?

Rousseau tried to snap Rick out of his melancholy mood. Rousseau was the Black hustler, lean, tall, always humming a song, always reminding people that he was three quarters French, Creole. "Rousseau, that's *French*," he'd say proudly.

"Man, oh, man, wake up. It's New Year's Eve. You're a million miles away," said Rousseau straddling the chair opposite Rick.

"Oh, hello, Rousseau," said Rick.

"What's on your mind. Such heavy thinking?"

"Money, what else?"

"Is that all? Your worries are over."

"Wish it were that simple."

"It is."

"Oh, come on, Rousseau."

"Listen. I gotta a proposition. See that old guy near that water fountain? His name's Marshall. Nice fellow. You know how he gets his kicks? He likes to watch two guys make love. He had told me almost a week ago that he wanted an all-night New Year performance. I had fixed up everything. You know that blond kid Yancey, the one who dresses like an ex-marine?"

"No."

"Yes, you do. You even told me that he's got nice buns."

"No, I don't know this Yancey."

"Well, never mind. Yancey has not shown up. He's late by nearly an hour. Marshall's getting impatient because he doesn't want to drive when it gets very dark. So, you want to step in Yancey's place? Make some money, spend New Year's Eve in a nice warm room, have some dinner, some drinks. What do you say?"

"How much does it pay?"

"I'll split even with you, whatever I get. Maybe ten, maybe fifteen, maybe twenty. Whatever we get, it's more than what we have now. Believe me, New Year's Eve is not good to score. What do you say?" Rousseau persuaded.

"Might as well, not much use sitting here," said Rick.

Rousseau introduced him to Marshall. They walked a little and then got into Marshall's car. Rousseau and Marshall in front, Rick in the back.

"You got any booze in your pad, Pop?" Rousseau asked.

"No. But we'll pick some up. What do you like?" Marshall asked.

"Some cognac for me. Rick, what do you like?" Rousseau asked.

"Nothing," said Rick.

"Good for you," Marshall said catching Rick's reflection in the mirror. "Your buddy's a nice looking kid."

"Wait till you see all of him, Pop. You'll cream in your pants. He's got the biggest thickest cock you've ever seen," Rousseau said.

The roads were slippery, and Marshall had a hard time driving. "Hey, Pop, turn those wheels over to me. I know how to drive on these roads. Here, move over," Rousseau said. Marshall moved the car to a side, stopped, and Rousseau maneuvered himself into the old man's place, as the old man moved to Rousseau's place.

Rousseau drove steadily. "See what I mean," he said.

They passed a few liquor stores, but there was no place to park. The roads were slippery and the cops were taking no chances by having cars stop even for a few minutes. Looking at this situation, Rousseau said, "Pop, next time we see a liquor store, you get off and buy some booze, while we go around the block and then come back to pick you up. Okay?"

"Sure," said Marshall.

They reached a store which was pretty crowded, and Marshall got out. Rousseau turned around the corner to go around the block.

"Real lousy weather," said Rick.

"What do you expect man, California sunshine?"

"Ah, that's where I want to go. California!" said Rick. "You took the words right out of my mouth, that's where I really want to go."

"Me too," said Rousseau.

"Have you ever been there, Rousseau?"

"No. Never enough money or company. I like someone to talk to on a long drive like that. A car, a guy, and a little money. I never had all three to make it to California," said Rousseau, stopping the car for the pedestrians to cross.

"You got a car and a guy, but no money," said Rick.

"What do you say we just take off for California?" asked Rousseau.

"Sure, but how?"

"How? Drive this car. Yeah, hold, on boy, we're on our way to sunny California."

"Sure, Rousseau. Take off."

Rick leaned back, closed his eyes, and sort of tried to drift into sleep or semi-sleep. "Hey, Rousseau, let me tell you one thing. I'm in no mood for sex tonight, so if I don't go crazy over you for the old man to watch, just fake it, okay," said Rick, still with his eyes closed.

"What'd you say? Come over in the front seat," said Rousseau. Rick opened his eyes, and climbed over.

"Hey, where we goin?" asked Rick, noticing that Rousseau was driving along without turning around any block.

"Where else? To Los Angeles."

"You're kidding?"

"No, I'm not. That's where I'm going. That's where you want to go?"

"Sure, but not in a stolen car!"

"Who said anything about stealing? I'm borrowing it, use it and return it to the old man, that is, if I find him," said Rousseau.

"I'm going to get off, Rousseau," said Rick.

"Why? Chicken? Listen, I need you, need some company. I've been wanting to go there myself, but never made up my mind. We can't plan, people like us, we got to take things as they come. Nothing will happen, we won't get caught. Relax," said Rousseau.

"What about the old man?"

"The old man? It'll be a long time before Marshall will know that we've taken his car. I've known him for almost three years. Never suspects that I can do something like this. So he'll wait, then he'll think maybe we've had an accident, so by the time he really decides to report the matter, we'll be way out, way out. Further, his heap isn't the best car in the world, probably worth a couple of hundred bucks at most. The old man'll think twice before reporting. He don't want to answer all kinds of awkward questions, you know," said Rousseau.

"What about gas out to California? What about money?" asked Rick.

"She's filled up now. The old man filled her up just before we got to the cafeteria. And as for money, we'll pick up some on the way— you know, you show your meat, I shake my butt. We'll make out okay. Take it easy. Sit back, relax, dream of Los Angeles and sandy beaches."

"I still got a few things at the Y," said Rick.

"Come on, Rick, all you got is a toothbrush and some old clothes. We'll pick up whatever you need on the way. This is a chance in a lifetime, so let's go."

"Okay, Rousseau, okay. Let's go," said Rick.

"We *are* going."

They drove all through the night, stopping just once at a drive-in for some coffee, and in the early morning reached Cleveland, Ohio. They parked near the Greyhound Bus Depot, washed up in the men's room, and had some breakfast. After Rick paid, he said, "Rousseau, all I got left is thirty-two cents."

"I got two-and-a-half bucks. We'll make it last till we get to Detroit," said Rousseau, taking the wheel again.

"Why Detroit?"

"I know a hotel in Detroit, pure queer trade there. I know the bellhop, that is, if he's still there. Maybe he can introduce us to a couple of customers, pick up some money, and then hit the road again," said Rousseau.

They kept driving, Rousseau talking all the way, describing all his adventures in Detroit, and New York, since he got there fifteen years ago from Baton Rouge. Singing and laughing, and totally carefree, he infused a new confidence and cheerfulness in Rick. Rick developed a liking for Rousseau.

They reached Detroit late in the evening, for Rousseau took the wrong route several times. They were both tired and hungry, ate hamburgers at a drug store, and Rousseau called the hotel. The bellhop was on night duty and was not supposed to be at the hotel until around ten. Rousseau was unable to get the phone number of the place he stayed.

"I'm glad he's still there," said Rousseau. "We have to wait for another two hours at least until I can get him," he added.

They parked the car, walked around the streets, and Rousseau called back. His friend was glad to hear Rousseau's voice, and asked him to give him the phone number of the booth he was calling from. A few minutes later he called back.

"I can use your white buddy," said his friend.

So they went to the hotel. Rousseau's friend the bellhop was also Black. He looked Rick over, and took him up in the elevator, and introduced him to an executive type looking guy. "Hope you have a good time, sir," the bellhop said. The executive tipped the bellhop, and shut the door after him.

"What's your name?" the executive asked Rick.

"Whatever you want to call me," said Rick.

"You remind me of a boy I loved in highschool, years ago. I'll call you Kenny," he said.

"I'm Kenny," Rick said and shook hands with the man.

"Go take a nice shower, use lots of soap. Clean out your asshole. I want to eat it," the man said.

Rick took a nice hot shower and used lots of soap as the man had suggested. He felt clean and refreshed. When he came out the man was lying on the bed nude with an erection.

"Blow me," the man said.

"No. You blow me," said Rick.

The man got up and gripped Rick's thighs and started to suck him. Then he turned Rick over and spread his legs and reamed him out. It excited him.

"I want to fuck you, okay?" the man asked.

"It'll cost you twenty-five bucks," said Rick. "I've never been fucked before," he added.

"Sure," the man said and applied some cream to Rick and savagely mounted him.

After it was over, Rick took another shower and came and dressed, and accepted the thirty bucks the man gave him.

"Aren't you going to count?" the man asked.

"I trust you," said Rick, eager to leave.

"It's just that I added a five dollar tip," the man said.

"Thanks, that's generous of you," said Rick.

"You're a great fuck. Just great," the man said and tried to kiss Rick. Rick pulled away.

"I'm here every Saturday night. Give me a call next Saturday night and we'll do it again," the man said.

"Sure, I'll do that," Rick said, and left.

Rousseau was waiting for him in the hotel coffee shop.

"How did it go?" he asked.

"Okay. I let him suck me."

"How much did you make?"

"Ten bucks," Rick said.

"He was supposed to give you fifteen."

"Maybe the bellhop took five bucks for his intro."

"The guy was supposed to give that separately. Shit, you should have demanded fifteen," said Rousseau.

"I didn't want any hassle," Rick said.

"Well, I got five for introducing you to the bellhop. So we got twenty between ourselves. That'll keep us going," said Rousseau.

"Yes, it will," said Rick.

They were dead tired by the time they reached Chicago. Rousseau wanted to drive on after a short stop, but Rick insisted they spend a couple of nights in Chicago by taking a room at the Y. Rick even wondered if they ought to drive to Clinton, just drive around the square, but did not pursue the idea.

In Chicago they tried to hustle, but except for a quickie at the Greyhound Bus Depot on Randolph Street, they had no luck. Rousseau suggested hitting a few bars, and Rick unwillingly accompanied him. But in the very first one, Rousseau got roaring drunk and Rick knew he was going to make a scene. He left Rousseau in the bar and came out. It was blistering cold and the windchill factor was unbearable. Rick went to a movie on Clark Street. In the washroom of the movie house, a tall, rangy, cowboy type propositioned him. They came out and went to a hotel room.

"My name's Tex, and I'm from Phoenix," the man said.

"Take me out to Phoenix," Rick said.

"Sure, boy, sure," Tex said.

They made love. Tex was tender and gentle and Rick enjoyed their session.

Next morning Rick was on his way to Phoenix with Tex. Tex did not drive at night. He would stop at a motel, they would have dinner and Tex would make love to Rick, saying very romantic things. It took them nearly five days by the time they reached Phoenix.

"I sure enjoyed your company, Rick," said Tex, stopping on West Camel Back Road in downtown Phoenix. He let Rick out and gave him ten dollars.

Tex had behaved like a perfect gentleman and Rick felt lonely as he saw him drive away.

Rick took a room at the Y, got a haircut, and spent the day in Phoenix. Next morning he checked out, hoping to hitchhike to L.A. or as close to L.A. as he could get. He walked over to a gas station, and stood in a corner hoping to get a ride. For nearly an hour or more he tried, raising his thumb, but with no luck. Then he saw a Volkswagen with a young, clean-cut blond guy fill up at the gas station. The young guy got out, and Rick noticed that he was well built and wearing a pink knit shirt and a pair of tight white tennis shorts. He saw the guy go to the washroom and wondered if he should go too, but decided to stay put. The guy came out, and he was a healthy attractive stud, thought Rick. As he got into the car and drove towards the street, Rick raised his thumb again, not at all in the least bit hopeful that the Volkswagen would stop. So he was very surprised when it did stop.

"Where are you headed?" the guy in the car asked.

"Los Angeles, or wherever you're going," said Rick.

"That's where I'm headed too. Get in," the guy said.

Rick got in.

"I'm Jeff."

"I'm Rick."

"Where you from, Rick?"

"New York."

"New York! I've always wanted to go there, maybe I will someday," Jeff said. Then he started to tell Rick that he was going to L.A. to see his girlfriend, and started to describe at great length the beauty and endowments of his girlfriend. He also started to describe what he'd done to several girls, and how every girl was after his hot body. "Boy, this time when I see Debbie, that's my girlfriend, I'm really going to ram it down her wet pussy," he said getting all excited.

Rick listened patiently.

"I bet all my sex talk has got you excited," Jeff said. "I bet you've had some hot girls in New York."

"No. I go for boys," Rick said to shock Jeff.

"No kidding. You're gay. Shake on it, I'm gay too. At last I can tell someone. Oh, God, that's terrific," said Jeff with excitement and pulled over and stopped his car.

Rick shook hands with Jeff.

"I put on this big male act, you know. I go to college, and live in this frat house, so I got to talk this eat-pussy talk. Big shit. But I hate the whole goddamn lot of those beer-drinking, cursing, swearing, conniving bastards," Jeff burst out. "You don't know how good it is to meet someone like you and say to you I'm gay. I hate girls. I love boys. God, I love you," Jeff said and hugged Rick.

"Take it easy, Jeff. Easy," said Rick overwhelmed by Jeff's emotional outburst.

"All these hot juicy hunks in my frat house, walking around bare chested, bareassed or in those sexy sweaty jockstraps! I go nuts seeing them all. And my roommate, the cutest kid you ever saw, slim and hung and god, those lips he's got. And you know, each morning he wakes up bareassed and with a morning hardon. Oh, to suck that dick. Just suck out all that fresh thick cream. You got a big cock, Rick? Hey, come on, please, let me see it, please," Jeff talked in rapid fire excitement.

"Cool it, please. We're on a public road," Rick said.

"I tell you what. Let's stop at the next motel and we'll have some fun. Okay? Then I'll drive you to Los Angeles right to the spot where you want to get off. Okay?"

"Let's go to Los Angeles, first. Then we'll get a hotel and we'll make love," said Rick.

"You bet we'll make love. That's the least you can do for this free ride you're getting all the way to El Lay," said Jeff.

"Sure, Jeff. Sure, you just take me to Los Angeles," said Rick.

They stopped in Yuma to eat. But Jeff was eager to take a look at Rick's meat, so he persuaded him to go to the washroom so he could get a "peek" at Rick's cock. When Rick unbuttoned and took out his meat, Jeff got very excited and wanted to get down on his knees and suck him right there. But Rick pulled back and caressed Jeff's round buns and said, "Let's get to a hotel and I'll give you the best fuck you've ever had."

"But I've never been fucked," said Jeff.

"Then it'll be the thrill of your lifetime," said Rick as he buttoned back his dungarees.

"You want to see my dick?" Jeff asked.

"In the hotel," said Rick squeezing Jeff's crotch.

Jeff bought Rick a great big meal, and watched him cut into his thick filet mignon. "Boy, even the way you eat, it's so damn sexy," said Jeff.

They started to drive and Jeff kept telling all the things he would do once they reached San Diego and took a hotel room.

"Why San Diego?"

"That's where I have to stop. But you'll love that town. All those sailors, from all over the world, in those damn tight pants. Just love to watch them."

"But you will take me to Los Angeles?"

"I promise. We'll spend the night in San Diego, and in the morning I'll drive you to El Lay," said Jeff.

They made it to San Diego late in the evening. They took a room in a nice hotel. Jeff could hardly wait to shut the door and hug Rick. He practically ripped Rick's clothes off. They fell on the bed nude and made love. Jeff had a healthy smooth tanned body and Rick enjoyed making love to this fresh exciting boy. Jeff gagged on Rick's throbbing endowment and screamed with joy when Rick fucked him. But Jeff was virtually insatiable, and it was after five bouts that he finally slept. Rick, too, was exhausted, but felt like smoking, and looked in Jeff's pockets. There were no smokes. He then looked in the airline bag that Jeff had brought with him, and found among the swim trunks and gym shorts a gun. He did not know whether it was loaded, but didn't touch it. Rick was fearful of Jeff now. Rick did not want to get involved in any kind of trouble. He had come this far, and now he did not intend messing it up. The sight of the gun really frightened him. Without making even the slighest noise, he dressed, and came out of the room carrying his shoes. He put them on in the corridor and walked towards the elevator, but returned again to the room, and pulled out the wallet fom Jeff's tennis shorts. There was a hundred and forty dollars. Rick took the five twenties, put the wallet back, came out and went down in the elevator. "Damn it, I've given him more than a hundred dollars of pleasure," thought Rick as he came out on the street.

It was four A.M. He walked toward the bus depot, and found that there was a non-stop express to Los Angeles in an hour. He had two cups of coffee in the coffee shop, bought a ticket and got on the bus. A few minutes after the bus started, Rick fell asleep in one of the back seats.

11

H E WOKE UP AS THE BUS entered Los Angeles and was rather disappointed to be introduced to the city by way of Mission Street, where all he saw were bums and drunks sleeping on pavements, and rather run-down buildings. Was this the glamour city, he wondered. Anyway, he was here at last, come to conquer the movie world. He laughed to himself at the unreality of it all.

As usual he went up from the bus depot looking for the Y, which was a rather dilapidated structure, and took a room, paying a week's rent, since he got a discount rate. He slept, took a shower and came out in the brilliant sunshine of Los Angeles. It was a clear day, and there was no smog. He had hoped that he'd bump into film stars when he came out, but L.A. was like any other city, except that it was warm and sunny. He walked along the streets, bought some toilet articles, picked up a pair of tight faded jeans and a couple of T-shirts in the Salvation Army Store. He was thrilled to see the long line of movie houses on Broadway, and was soon busy scanning the various signs to see what he had not seen. There were quite a few.

He relaxed for a couple of days in L.A. and soon realized that the eternal problem had to be faced—the problem of money, of survival.

He did not find it easy to find customers for his body. He began to haunt the couple of doughnut shops, an all-night restaurant, the bus depot, and, of course, Pershing Square in downtown L.A. But business was bad, and the police seemed to be more vigilant here than in any other place. The Square, or the Park, as hustlers called it, was interesting to Rick for the first couple of days. He heard that Hollywood was a good place to hustle, but Rick needed some money and some decent clothes to get there. The bus fare itself cost a buck to get to Hollywood and return.

So he wandered in the park, picking up a few old men who were ravenous wth their lust but tight with money. He felt very dirty after these quickie jobs behind bushes or in sleazy movie houses. When his rent ran out, he stayed with a toothless old man for a couple of nights, but left, for the man was ugly, dirty and poor. He remembered Andy with nostalgia, wondering how his life might have been if he had stayed on with him, and even possibly managed that clothing store.

He again moved into a dollar-a-day room, walking from morning till evening in the park, round and round until he got tired, and then sitting down on one of the park benches, getting up and moving away only when he saw the cops, for fear he might be questioned and picked up for lewd vagrancy.

Nearly a month passed in this way, and that morning he got up as usual, hoping he'd make more than the few dollars he was making a day. But the morning and evening turned out as usual, and Rick knew that today would be but a repetition of other days of misery. He had not even made a dollar, and all he had was fifty cents in his pocket, which he held onto however hungry he was, for if nothing came his way before midnight, he could at least spend the fifty cents by sitting in an all-night movie house and get some sleep.

He sat in the park, close to a group that gathered every Friday evening and sang everything from "Sweet Adeline" to "Jesus Will Save You." He watched the subtle glances of the persons in that group as they tried to make the contact, and hoped that someone would notice him. It was these clothes, he thought to himself, that made him look so shabby and skinny. He needed some new clothes, even just a pair of tight dungarees so that, as Jake had told him a long time ago, he could package his meat for proper display. He pulled at his trousers, and noticed how loose and baggy they had become. He had lost weight, no doubt.

Soon he became aware of a man watching him, and looked at him with a smile. The man moved away, stopping a little way down. Rick got up and followed him. They got out of the park, and crossed the street to the other side. But just as Rick got onto the other side of the street, he noticed a white and yellow Plymouth Fury stop on his side of the street for the lights to change. The prosperous middle-aged man driving the car looked at Rick. And Rick knew the meaning of that stare, of the flash of desire.

The lights changed, the car moved, but Rick hoped that the man would circle the park and come back again. He wanted someone like that, someone who was prosperous. And the man in that sleek car meant nothing else but prosperity. Maybe he was even a movie star, thought Rick.

Meanwhile the man who had cruised him in the park came up to him. He asked Rick for a match.

"No match, but I got something you want," said Rick, looking at the end of the street to see if the Plymouth was coming back.

"You sure don't waste any time," the man said.

"What's the use? I've wasted a lot of time."

"Let's go."

"How much?"

"Well, what can I expect from you?"

Rick's face brightened, for the Plymouth was coming, and he did not answer the man next to him.

"Come on, fellah," the man said.

"Just a minute," Rick said, as the car came closer. Rick stared at the man inside the car. The man stopped the car, opened the window, and asked, "How do you get to Hollywood?"

Rick heard the question, yet he asked, "What?" and went to the car.

"Get in. Want a ride?" the man asked.

Rick was in the car before the man had completed asking the question. The man was in his forties, but had a trim muscular build. Rick was surprised to see him in a pair of white swim shorts.

"Been at the beach all day," the man explained. "Where are you from?" he asked.

"Here and there."

"Looking for a job?"

"Sure."

"What kind?"

"Anything that pays well."

"Like some music?"

"Why not?"

The man turned on the radio and got some light dance music.

"Where are we going?" Rick asked.

"To a drive-in."

"Listen, I don't want to see any movie."

"Who does? We'll just get acquainted, then go to my nice place. You like to swim?"

"Of course. You got a pool?"

"A nice outdoor pool."

"Sounds great."

"How long can you stay with me?"

"As long as you want. I got nothing urgent."

"Good," the man said as he patted Rick's thighs.

"You think we can stop for a burger or something? I'm real starved," said Rick.

"Sure, we'll get something at the snack bar in the drive-in. Okay?"

"Sure."

The man spoke softly and gently, and looked like a nice person. Rick hoped he'd be able to stay with him for a few days, get some good food, rest, swim in that nice pool of his. And if the car was any indication, then the man probably had a nice well-furnished place.

They did not talk on the way, but every time their eyes met, the man smiled pleasantly. They reached a drive-in, and went in, parking in a sparsely populated section. Some movie dealing with gang warfare was going on. The man put his arms around Rick, dragging him close, held him like that for a minute, then his hand slid down. "Slip it off, kid," he whispered.

"Here?" Rick asked.

"Sure, this is what excites me."

Rick eased out of his dungarees. The man stroked Rick's meat. "Big boy," he said. Then he wiggled out of his shorts and asked Rick to suck him. Rick obeyed and got the man hard. The man turned Rick around and fucked him, coming quickly.

"I was all worked up," the man explained and handed Rick some tissues.

Rick wiped himself and eased back into his dungarees.

"I feel much better now," the man said putting his shorts on.

"Let's go to your place and I'd like to take a shower and get some food. I feel real dirty," Rick said.

"Sure. I like you. You're so agreeable."

They came out of the drive-in, and silently drove on. The man pulled into a large shopping area on the way and said to Rick, "Do me a favor. Please get me a pack of cigarettes. Anything mentholated will do," and handed Rick a dollar.

Rick got out and went to a large grocery store nearby. There was quite a line at the check out counter, but when Rick came out, the man and the car were gone. Oh, shit, he cursed to himself. What Rick and Rousseau had done to the old man in New York, now had happened to him here in California.

He stood there, completely miserable, not knowing where he

was. He was too weak even to work up an anger.

He thought of asking someone where exactly he was, how far from downtown L.A. He spotted a guy in a bright red T-shirt and army fatigues struggling with an armful of groceries. Rick went up to him and said, "Here, let me give you a hand."

"Gee, thanks," the fellow said, handing Rick some of the stuff. "I don't know why I didn't get a shopping cart," the man explained as they walked to his car.

"Could you tell me where we are?" Rick asked.

"Glendale."

Rick had a blank expression. "How far is that from downtown L.A.?" he asked.

"Quite a way," the fellow replied. "What's the matter? You look lost," he added, seeing Rick.

"Yeah, I am lost. I came with a fellow, but I can't find him now. And I don't know how to get back," Rick said.

"Oh, one of those practical jokers, eh? Well, hop in, I'll drop you off in L.A.," the fellow said.

"Thanks. I hate to trouble you," Rick said.

"One good turn deserves another," the fellow said driving.

Rick wondered if he could make a pass at this athletic looking guy. But he didn't look gay, but then what about Jeff who looked and talked so tough, but who turned out to be as gay as they come? Anyway, he'd see, send out a feeler, Rick thought.

They drove in silence for about fifteen minutes, then Rick asked the fellow where he was going.

"Drop you off, and get home."

"What do you do at home?"

"Oh, you know, maybe watch TV, fix something to eat, read, then sack out."

"Is that all?"

"Why? Is there anything else I ought to be doing?"

"Yes. You should have some fun."

"Oh, I do. But not tonight. I keep that kind of activity for the weekends, if you know what I mean," the man said smiling.

"Why not tonight?"

"Gee, I don't get you," said the fellow looking at Rick.

Rick reached out and squeezed the fellow's thighs. The fellow jumped as though a scorpion had stung him. "God dammit, you son of a bitch. You damn queer, get the hell out of . . ." He stopped the car abruptly and literally pushed Rick out, and drove off in a rage.

Well, he had tried. Rick continued to walk for some time, and asked a passerby how he could get to Pershing Square.

"Keep walking till you come to Hill Street, then turn right," the man said.

It took him half an hour or more to get to Pershing Square. Completely exhausted in body and spirit, he sat on a stone bench. There were still people moving around, and Rick just sat, hoping that a cop would catch him and put him in prison, for that at least would give him some place to stay and some food.

He sat till midnight, but when he saw a cop coming to throw people out, Rick got up and left. As he was leaving the park, he met a lean, tall fellow.

"A lousy night for business," he said.

"You're telling me," Rick said.

They walked on, and the fellow said he was going to a movie house, saying that maybe he could pick up someone there. They walked to the Mexican side of the town and went into a movie house by paying thirty-five cents each. "Come up," the fellow said, and they went upstairs. There seemed to be more people in the washroom than in the theatre watching the show. Rick stood in front of a urinal, so did the tall fellow, both displaying themselves unashamedly. A burly Mexican with a big moustache came and patted Rick on the shoulder and said, "Hi, amigo."

"Go, kid, go," said the tall fellow next to him.

Rick was surprised that things were so open. He left with the Mexican and they bargained while the Mexican kept squeezing Rick's crotch. Finally Rick agreed to take five dollars for a fast job. They walked into the dark theatre, went up to the balcony and sat on the far left side of the last row.

No one interrupted the Mexican as he sucked on Rick's limp meat. Too many others were busy buying and selling flesh and desire. Too many other studs were warming up for a few hours before hustling out once again out on the cold streets.

The Mexican was disappointed that Rick could not get a hardon. He cursed him in Spanish and walked away. But fortunately this time Rick had collected his fee before he had unzipped.

Rick walked out of the theatre into the raw cold air. He was overwhelmed by a feeling of loneliness, hunger and despair. Dazed, tired, and gnawed at by futility, he began to walk the streets like a lost child, doomed to walk forever naked to the night.

12

THE FOLLOWING DAY PROVED EVEN WORSE. It was a Saturday, and the Park was filled with humpy young sailors from the nearby bases in San Diego and Long Beach. With their well-scrubbed looks, their tight white pants, and cocky good looks and their navy caps perched arrogantly on their heads, ooozing with virility, no one bothered to look at Rick. He took a look at himself in front of a shoe shop, and was startled to discover how haggard and shabby he had become. His eyes were red, his face pale and thin, and his clothes very dirty.

Around midnight, when the cops took up their beat in the park, Rick left, walking back and forth from Main Street to Broadway, pausing in front of closed shop windows if he sensed a slight interest on the part of some stranger.

His feet grew weary, and he stood on a corner on Broadway near a bus stop for a short rest. He saw a blond young fellow, dressed very neatly, interested in a young sailor who was standing near the bus stop. But the sailor stood indifferently, confident of his good looks and robust young body. Rick recalled how he, too, had walked so proudly, ignoring cruising looks. An elderly man dressed very stylishly in a dark suit joined the scene, standing closer to the sailor than the blond young man.

Now there were two, both interested in the sailor, and Rick hoped that the loser in this intimate pick-up drama would turn to pick *him* up. Rick moved closer to the blond, and with his hands in his pockets tried to work up an erection. The man in the stylish dark suit had already started his conversation with the sailor. The blond was disappointed when he saw the sailor and the dark-suited man walk away.

The blond stood for a minute, bit his nails, and turned to walk away. He caught sight of Rick, who smiled, but the blond ignored him and walked on. Desperately Rick followed him, catching him in a darker part of the street. "Hey, buddy, hey, just a minute, can I talk to you, please?"

The blond stopped.

"You want me?" Rick asked, directly, appealingly.

"Well . . ."

"I saw you watch the sailor. I'll give you a good time . . . I promise. I'm really hung, got a body, it's just these clothes . . ." Rick started and stopped feeling humiliated that he had come to this state where he had to literally sell himself.

The blond looked at Rick and said, "Well, I'm all worked up. Might as well take you. What do you charge?"

"I leave that up to you."

"No. Tell me. I don't want any trouble later. Okay. How much?"

"Honest, whatever you give. Okay. Come on, let's go," said Rick not wanting to lose the blond who looked neat and smelled of cologne.

They walked. At the end of the block, on the corner, the blond stopped at a car, an Austin Healey. Rick got in the car and waited until the blond entered and started the ignition.

Not one word did they speak in the car. Rick just leaned back and rested his head on the seat.

After nearly an hour or so of driving, the car pulled up, and the blond said, "Here we are."

Rick stepped out, while the blond parked the car in a garage. They climbed the stairs and got into the apartment. The blond put on all the lights, and looking at Rick said, "You do look tired. Go take a nice shower. I'll fix you an omelette."

When Rick walked into the bathroom, the blond shouted, "Feel free to use plenty of soap."

When Rick came out of the shower in a towel, the lights had been put out except for one over a low couch. The blond was stretched out on it wearing just a skimpy red and black bikini. He was smoking.

Rick sat on the floor and the blond pushed the plate of omelette and toast towards him. There was also a large glass of milk. Rick ate silently, enjoying the fluffy omelette.

"You feel better?" the blond asked.

"Much better. Thank you for bringing me," said Rick with genuine gratitude.

"That's okay. We're lonely people. We need each other's help."

They were silent for a minute. The blond got up. "Would you like some more milk?" he asked.

"No, thanks. This was delicious," Rick said.

The blond slowly eased out of his bikini. Slim, tight bodied and tanned all over except where he had worn the bikini, he excited Rick.

Rick stood up and dropped his towel.

They hugged and the blond said, "You weren't kidding when you said you were big," and caressed Rick's heavy low hung balls.

"You have such a nice body," Rick said as he licked the blond's nipples.

"What's your name by the way?"

"Rick."

"I'm Turk."

They walked into the bedroom and made passionate love.

He heard the sound of music and assayed the smell of fresh brewed coffee when he woke up. He took a minute to recollect where he was. He sat up in bed, looking around, then walked nude into the kitchen where Turk was fixing breakfast. He was wearing a pair of tight khaki shorts.

Rick went behind and hugged him hard and whispered in his ear, "Hi."

"Oh . . . you caught me by surprise." He turned around and they kissed. "Did you sleep well, Rick?" he asked.

"Best sleep I've had in months," Rick said.

"Good. I'm fixing breakfast. You want pancakes or waffles or just eggs?"

"Turk, whatever you fix is okay."

"No, tell me. I love to cook."

"Pancakes then," said Rick, going to the bathroom.

By the time he came out after a shower with a towel around his waist, Turk had set the breakfast table.

"I'm out of orange juice this morning, Rick," said Turk.

"That's okay," said Rick sipping the coffee. "Delicious," he said.

"Why didn't you wear those white gymshorts I had left for you in the bathroom?" Turk asked.

"Sorry. Were they for me?"

"Yes, they were for you. They're from my old prep school in New Hampshire."

Rick got up.

"You can wear them later. Sit down, enjoy your breakfast."

"Okay, Turk."

They ate in silence and then, as Turk poured some more coffee for Rick, he said, "I enjoyed last night. Very much."

"Me too. You are so gentle, so affectionate," said Rick.

"I haven't been fucked like that in a long while," said Turk.

"Thanks. I'm at your command," Rick said.

"What's your plan, Rick?"

"My plan? I have none. You ask me to leave, I'll leave. You saved my life last night. I mean that. I was in such a suicidal mood," Rick said.

"I'd like you to stay."

"I'd love to."

"Shall we go to the beach? Just right beach weather today."

"How far is the beach?"

"You can see it from the bedroom window. Didn't you notice?"

"No. Where are we anyway?"

"Santa Monica, right on the beach. I've been here for nearly eight years now, used to be in downtown L.A. But I like it here."

"What kind of work do you do, Turk? You don't have to tell me if you don't want to."

"That's no secret. I work as an assistant manager in a large music store on Hollywood Boulevard. Been there for nine years. Like it."

"How old are you, Turk?"

"Old enough . . . twenty-eight to be exact."

"Twenty eight? You look very young, nineteen, twenty maybe."

"Thanks. Yes, I have what my highschool year book described, 'the eternal boyish look'," said Turk, brushing back his abundant blond hair from his forehead. "You're . . . let me guess, nineteen?"

"Twenty."

They were silent again.

"I'll do the dishes later. Shall we go to the beach? Get some sun, unwind, that sort of thing?"

"Sure. But I got nothing to wear for the beach. My pants and T-shirt and jacket need to be burned. They're so filthy," said Rick.

"Wear those white gymshorts I left for you in the bathroom. Or would you prefer a nice stretch bikini?" Turk offered.

"The gymshorts would do," said Rick and walked to the bathroom to change. When he came out, Turk stared at him and said, "You want to borrow a jockstrap?"

Rick looked at himself and said, "Much too obvious?"

"I didn't mean it that way," said Turk.

"I guess it's okay," said Rick. "If I don't get a hardon," he added and laughed.

They walked towards the beach which was just a few minutes' walk. It was filled with people. The sun was glaring. They found a spot very close to the water and Turk spread out a large beach towel.

"This is California. This is the L.A. I thought of while I shivered in the winter of New York," said Rick, glancing at the brightly striped umbrellas and healthy bodies in colorful swimwear.

"If you walk *that* way," said Turk pointing, "you'll run into the famous muscle beach. That's where all the good looking muscleboys hang out. We'll take a look over there, later."

Turk started to read a paperback, and Rick went to take a dip in the water. It was only after he had waded into the water that he realized that he ought not to have done it, because the wet gymshorts clearly outlined the shape and size of his thick cock.

Turk looked at Rick going into the water, wondered for a moment what type of guy he really was, whether he could trust him, whether he could ask him to move in with him. Turk was fed up cruising and looking for one-night stands.

About half-an-hour later, Rick came running back, dripping wet and sat down quickly trying to cover himself with the towel. Several on the beach had looked at him and were making comments about his equipment.

"I should have put on a jock strap," Rick said.

Turk smiled and pulled the towel from under him and gave it to Rick.

Rick wrapped it around his waist and wiggled out of his wet gymshorts.

"Thanks for last night, Turk. I mean it," said Rick.

"I should thank you. I'm glad I did not pick up that sailor," he said.

"Me too."

They sat and chatted and relaxed. Turk read, and Rick dozed off on the sand.

"Hey, Rick, want to get a burger or something?" Turk asked.

"What?" Rick opened his eyes slowly.

"You want to get a bite to eat?" Turk asked.

"What time is it?"

"Ten-after-five," said Turk looking at his watch.

"That late?"

"Yeah. I'll go and get a couple of burgers and some milk from the muscle burger grill. Okay?" Turk got up.

"Let me come with you," said Rick.

They collected their things and walked over. On the way they stopped to watch the young men on that strip of sand called muscle beach, proudly displaying their pumped-up well-oiled bodies. Everyone was engaged in some form of activity designed to pay homage to the body beautiful.

Rick was fascinated with the sculptured physiques, all the grunting and groaning and the challenging cries from the onlookers egging on the weight lifters. "This is incredible," he said moving closer. "I feel so skinny looking at all these muscles," he said to Turk.

Turk had put on his dark sun glasses. "They're juicy, aren't they?" he said softly. "I like that short humpy guy over there. The light haired one in the tan colored bikini," he said, gesturing slightly with his head. Rick looked at the young blond boy who had attracted Turk's attention. With his bronzed body, and his corn blond hair bleached by the sun, his armorplate pecs and his tight firm buns, he was an adonis. He moved with pride and uninhibitedly displayed himself, flexing his biceps and doing squats to show off his powerful thighs. The tight bikini cleaved the cheeks of his buttocks and wisps of blond hair peeked out from his crotch.

"What a well stacked hunk. I'd give anything to get crushed and fucked by him," said Turk. "Come on, let's go," he added and they went to eat at the grill.

It was getting cooler. Turk suggested they get back to the apartment after they had eaten their burgers and fries. Rick wanted to linger around. So they returned to their original place on the sand.

"I sure go for the muscle-boy type," said Turk. "I'm turned on by nice pecs. Love to suck hard nipples."

"Go get one," said Rick, slightly hurt, becoming sensitive about his skinny looks.

"I wish I could, but it's hard to make the contact. I know you can make the contact. I know for a fact that the blond hunk is gay in spite of all his swagger, but I'm shy, I guess," said Turk.

"Why don't you join a gym? Put on muscles, then you'll be like one of them, and become buddies with these guys and next thing you'll be sucking these muscleboys," Rick said with a touch of sarcasm.

"I've tried that, believe me. But it's difficult," said Turk.

"Hard lifting weights? Sure, it's hard, but then you've heard the old saying, no pain, no gain."

"I used to have a permanent hardon when I worked out in a gym.

So I gave up pumping iron," said Turk.

Rick did not say anything.

"You know what, Rick?"

"What?"

"After studying literally hundreds of physiques, I've arrived at the perfect measurements for the best male figure," said Turk.

"You told me you were all excited just to see a muscle hunk, so how could you . . ."

"Physique pictures, you know."

"Huh?"

"When we get to the apartment I'll show you. I have a good collection," said Turk.

"Okay," said Rick and then very hesitantly asked, "Turk, how long do you want me to stay with you?"

Turk did not answer.

"That's all right. Feel free, Turk. You've given me a great day of rest, relaxation and terrific . . . sex. Food and friendship too. So, anytime you want me to leave, say the word," said Rick.

"It's not that. You see, I've never had a guy with me for longer than a night. I fight hard against attachment, because when it's broken, I find it hard, very hard to patch up the wound," he said with a keen sense of sadness in his voice.

Rick felt the impact of loneliness in that voice, he got up, and looking at Turk said, "You must have been hurt real bad."

"Bad enough," said Turk.

"Want to tell me?"

"It's a long story."

"I got time," said Rick.

"Maybe we should get back to the apartment. We'll have some coffee, and then if you're still interested, I'll confess," said Turk.

They got back to the apartment. Turk gave Rick another pair of olive colored shorts.

"Where are you from, Rick?" Turk asked as both sat in the living room drinking coffee.

"That's a long story too," said Rick.

"As you said, I got time, too. I've taken the day off, if you didn't notice," said Turk.

Slowly and hesitantly at first, but later compelled by the strong desire to confess, Rick told his story to Turk. Told everything except the incident where he had stolen from Jeff in the hotel in San Diego.

"You've really had a tough time, haven't you?" asked Turk after listening to Rick's story. Rick did not answer.

"Mine isn't so gruesome, but I've had my problems too," Turk said, lighting up a cigarette and reclining against the back of the couch.

"Go ahead, tell me about it," Rick said. "Misery loves company. And I'm your company," Rick said smiling.

Turk did not need any prodding. It was clear that he had been looking for a sympathetic ear into which he could pour his misadventures as an unhappy, frustrated homosexual in the straight world. From his seduction, the first time by his sister's boyfriend, to his dismissal from college after being found in bed with a sailor from a local base, Turk expanded on his lonely life.

"At least you didn't have to hustle," said Rick. "That's tough, I'll tell you."

"No, I didn't. A week after I finally hit L.A. I got a job in a cafeteria, cleaning the tables. It was rough work, and the manager was a regular son-of-a-bitch. But I held on for nearly two months there, then one day I saw this sign in the window of this music store in Hollywood, asking for a boy who'd be interested in a job. All I had to do was put back in place records that the customers had misplaced or pulled out to listen to. I liked it. There were a lot of customers coming and going, some very good looking guys too. So I stayed on. They've been good to me. Marty, the man who owned the store, died, but his son is equally pleasant. Given me raises, now I'm next to the manager. I often work overtime, and if once in a while I need to take a day off, I just call. No hassle."

"So you're content?" said Rick.

"Yes, though no man is fully content. I read, I listen to music, go to movies, plays. I have a few friends, but no one knows I'm gay. Or even if they know I'm gay, they don't pry or make fun of me. Twice a month, I pick up a guy, have sex, pay him. Once in a while I feel like having a steady boyfriend, but then I'm not sure if it'll work. Basically I'm a very private person. So that's my life in a nutshell," he said and added, "although it's a big nutshell since I've taken such a long time telling you."

"So, I'm sort of unique, right? I've been with you almost a day," said Rick.

"Yes, Rick. I think you're unique in some respects. Here, definitely," Turk said reaching for Rick's crotch.

"Ah, you're trying to tell me something," said Rick standing up.

"I want to suck you."

Rick eased down his gymshorts.

13

B Y SHARING THEIR EXPERIENCES with each other, Rick and Turk forged a strong bond emotionally and sexually. In the morning, Turk woke up earlier than Rick and did not know whether he should send Rick away, or have him stay at least for another day or two. He did not feel like waking Rick, but he had to go to work. He decided however that he would take another day off. He called his boss and took the day off.

Turk made breakfast, and waited for Rick to get up. Sitting in the living room, Turk wondered what he should do. Since yesterday he had developed a genuine fondness for Rick, and his first impulse was to ask him to stay, but then Rick was young, and had ambitions to pursue a film career. Of course everyone and anyone who came to L.A. always talked of getting into the movies, and there was only a one-in-a-million chance that Rick would make it. Yet Turk did not want to get hurt if Rick suddenly left him after he had become attached to him.

But Turk felt the loneliness of his life too, more than ever now, as he sat smoking. He walked over to the bedroom and watched Rick sleeping. He was a handsome hunk, hypnotic black eyes, long dark eyelashes, a bit skinny, but with a bone structure that was quite big enough to put on flesh and muscles. Then that enormous cock and those big balls. Suddenly Turk smiled, for he got what he thought was an excellent idea. He wondered if it would work. No harm in trying. At least for the success of this experiment he would ask Rick to stay. It would take a long time, but it was worth it. Yes, he would have Rick work out in the gym, and put on muscles, so that Turk could sculpt Rick into becoming his own, his very own, muscle boy.

Turk was so turned on by the idea that he woke Rick up.

"Rick, I've got a tremendous idea, just great," he said, sitting on the bed, and gently caressing Rick's nude back.

"Take it easy, let me get some coffee," said Rick, still drowsy, but getting off the bed and going into the bathroom.

Turk hurried into the kitchen and brought out the breakfast. Rick came out. "Boy, you sure are excited."

"Wait till you hear this, come sit down," said Turk.

Rick reached for the coffee cup.

"Rick, how would you like to be my own muscle boy?"

"What?"

"You see, I was just thinking, looking at you, while you were sleeping. You are a really good looking stud . . ."

"Oh, yes. I've heard that before. Handsome, but dead broke," interrupted Rick cynically.

"Listen, willya? Of course you look a little tired and skinny, but you have a terrific frame for muscles. Look at that broad chest and shoulders, the narrow hips, and hung like a horse," said Turk.

"Continue, sounds good," said Rick.

"Of course, looking at me you'd say that I knew nothing about weight lifting. But I do. That's my passion, my hobby. I'll soon show you my collection of physique pictures. I know what exercise to do to develop a certain muscle, how many sets, where to double up on your weights, where not to, what routines to follow, what kind of food to eat, how to give that satiny look to your skin, oh, heck, I could go on. If I had the determination to use all I know about muscle building in building my own muscles, I'd be the handsomest hunk of gorgeous blond meat walking around," said Turk.

"Why don't you?"

"I told you, Rick, I can't. The moment I go to a gym and watch all those guys with muscles, I get so horny, I told you. But, you see, I could give you all this instruction. I'd feed you the right foods, the right meats and fish, fresh salads, oh, everything to trim and shape that body of yours. I have a life membership in a gym. I've never used it after a few visits. You could use it. Just remember your name is Turk Harrison while you're in the gym, that's all. You start working out three times a week. Get a nice tan on the beach. No work to do. Get up late, eat a hearty breakfast, just laze in the sun, and turn into a golden hunky Adonis. What more do you want? I'll have a goal: to shape my own, my very own muscleboy, a sort of a patron to a superguy. Lesson one: take one dark-eyed, very handsome, very well hung horny hunk like Rick," said Turk. He laughed, moved closer to Rick, dragged him close and kissed him.

Rick smiled back, but went on eating.

"What do you say, Rick? What do you say?"

"Let's see your pictures," said Rick.

"Sure," said Turk and brought out a large-sized leather box from the bedroom closet.

Stacked up in neat bundles were physique magazines and albums full of male models. Soon Turk was busy showing and commenting on these pictures. He told how so-and-so was when he was only seventeen, how improved he was at twenty-one. Turk admired the pumped up pectorals of one, and the round firm melon buttocks of another, and lingered over the muscular thighs of yet another. Then he opened his albums to show his collection of pictures from all over the world. Some were clothed in a fig leaf, but there were quite a few models in all their glorious nudity.

There was one album that had photos of famous movie stars, an album that interested Rick. Rick was surprised to see some of the handsome, popular teenage movie stars so robust, naked and showing off in their revealing poses. "Gosh, how did you get these?" Rick asked in appreciative amazement. Turk was pleased with the compliment. He had never shown his collection to anyone, not a soul, so that now, sharing it with Rick, he felt happy, and excited.

"So this is how Rad looks without his tight pants," said Rick, admiring the picture of a young teenage singer who was the current rage. "Never knew he was so grand inside," Rick added. "Where did you get this picture?" he asked.

Turk smiled. "I'll let you in on my secret," he said. "See this?" he said, pointing to Rad's face. "It's cut out and pasted to this body. And this body belongs to a terrific model. I like Rad's face, and the model's body, so I joined the two."

"What do you know? You never can tell," said Rick, holding up the picture to examine it carefully.

Turk had done it all, though, a face to fit a body, and a body to fit a face. There was no doubt that he had spent time, energy and money in building up this hobby. Now he wanted to experiment with a real person. "You got the stunning face, all you need is the body," said Turk.

"Gosh, Turk, you've spent hours on this project. But it's great," said Rick.

"Thanks."

Rick went on looking through the photos and the magazines. Turk gazed longingly at Rick. "What do you say, Rick? Will you agree to stay and let me train you to develop a first rate hot body?" Turk asked.

"Okay, Turk. I got nothing else to do," said Rick.

"You mean that?" Turk asked excitedly.

"Sure."

"Let's seal our deal with a kiss," said Turk.

"Just with a kiss? Look what these photos have done to me," said Rick revealing his bulge.

"I can take care of that," said Turk.

Rick fell back as Turk unzipped Rick's pants.

14

T HEY WENT TO THE BEACH, Rick wearing a skimpy bikini that Turk had loaned to him. On the way Rick dropped a brown shopping bag in a garbage can.

"What was that?" asked Turk.

"My dirty pants and T-shirt. All I now own is an old jacket which is in your apartment, and this bikini which really belongs to you," said Rick.

"What are you trying to say?"

"That I'm truly naked in the world."

"You look much better in the nude than in clothes," said Turk.

"Oh, shut up," Rick said, playfully trying to hit Turk who ran. Rick raced him to the beach.

Later that day, Turk bought Rick a new pair of levis and gave him a sweat shirt of his own, and persuaded him to start going to the gym.

"I'll go tomorrow, Turk."

"You can't go tomorrow. You'll have to go Wednesday, and that means half this week is over. Just go, look around, you don't have to lift all the weights today. Come on, let me take you," persuaded Turk. "But remember that you are Turk Harrison, I'm Rick. Wish I were," he said, giving Rick his membership card.

It was a plush gym, red carpeted, piped in music, steam bath, sun lamp room, swimming pool, the works. Rick felt embarrassed working out, as his skinny body was reflected in all the mirrors around the big hall. Turk watched the muscle boys. Within half an hour, Rick had decided to leave.

"Just follow my instructions and the mirror'll reflect you gloriously," encouraged Turk as they left the gym.

So started Rick's muscle building program. Turk outlined the type of exercises that Rick had to do, and prepared the nutritious foods Rick needed.

Rick settled down to a routine. He'd get up late, for he became a TV addict and watched the late late shows, long after Turk had gone to sleep. Then he'd have his breakfast, and laze around. He'd go to the gym, work out, come back, have lunch and lie on the beach bronzing himself. He even started reading some books, novels, that were in the apartment and that Turk recommended. Evenings, when Turk returned, they would talk, and Turk would fix a good meal. Then it would be going to the movies or watching TV or walks or jogging by the beach.

It was a very relaxing life, and Rick came to like it. He even enjoyed going to the gym, and working up a good sweat. He liked to stretch and pull at his muscles, lie on his back and push up the weights, and feel the keen sense of pain in the joints. He liked particularly those buddy exercises where he worked out with another guy, who sat on his back making him raise his legs to develop his calf muscles, or straddle his leg to make Rick stretch way back to give definition to his torso. At times, when the weights became heavy, and the last set of exercises the toughest, and Rick required all his energy, the pain of pressure became a touch of ecstasy. Rick reveled in it.

After a couple of months, during dinner one evening, Turk said that Rick ought not to wear scanty clothes any more in front of him. Rick was just wearing a pair of tight grey shorts.

"Don't tell me you don't want to look at me?"

"God, I do. That's why. I notice that your body is now ready to take on the flesh and definition of muscles. But you know, Rick, I want to see you fully naked a year from now, no less than a year I should say. I met you, let me see, on March nineteenth, and you started at the gym on March twenty-first. So I'll see you on March twenty-first next year. I'll inaugurate or unveil my statue-come-to-life then. I want to keep up the suspense of seeing you."

"You know, Turk, I think you're a bit crazy. Not always, but sometimes," said Rick laughing.

"Okay. So I'm crazy. But will you just do as I say? Please?" said Turk.

"Yes, Master. I'll dress as though it's freezing winter," said Rick.

"Don't wear tight pants. Wear something loose, baggy."

"Okay, okay. Get me what you want me to wear, okay?"

"I will. Now, I have to make another sacrifice to see that you become one of the best built hunks. This will be tough," said Turk.

"What's that?"

"I gotta give up all my passionate love making with you. Mustn't drain your life juices by sucking your cock. Comprende?"

"You mean that?"

"I do."

"This turning me into an Adonis has really got you, hasn't it?"

"Did you ever doubt that?"

"So what are you going to do when you get a hardon?"

"I've been thinking of that too, Rick. Here's where I need your understanding. I'll have to go cruising and pick up a one night stand. I know that's tough, go in search of cheap candy while I have honey right at home. I hope you don't mind, Rick. It's just to get my rocks off. You're my true love," said Turk.

Rick smiled and said, "I understand. Just let me know when you're humping or getting humped by a hustler, I'll stay right in my room. And if ever he treats you rough, I'll come out and bash his brains," said Rick, and tousled Turk's blond hair.

"Thank you, my adorable protector," said Turk.

This strange love affair continued. Turk bought some real baggy sweat pants and sweat shirt for Rick to wear at home. He also started talking to Rick not only about the finer points of body building, but introduced him to good music of which Turk knew quite a bit, recommended some good books for Rick to read. So apart from moulding his body, Turk attempted to bring into Rick's life some good culture as well.

Rick developed a few friends, too, outside the apartment. There was Otto, the gorgeous blond kid at muscle beach, who, like Rick, had a private sugar daddy and spent time on the beach flexing his muscles and bronzing his body. There was Rita, a young divorcee who hung around the beach, acting as errand girl to the muscle boys, bringing them stuff to eat, or oiling their bodies or acting as hostess whenever there was a beach party. She was also the available girl to be tossed about by athletes in the tumbling acts they used to practice on the beach.

But Rita was more than that. She had a reputation for giving super blow jobs to some of the guys. She wanted Rick since she knew that beneath that bulge Rick had a tool she wanted to suck. Often she would spread the suntan lotion on his broad back, and chat with him as he lay on the beach.

"I bet you're a virgin," she said to Rick one day.

"Why do you say that?"

"I mean, I know you've shacked up with a lot of guys, but never with a girl. Right?"

Rick remained silent.

Rita was an outspoken young girl. "Hey, listen, there's nothing wrong with that. A lot of guys here prefer guys. But a few of the guys who think they're completely gay get a taste of my mouth and realize that they can swing both ways. If you want to give it a try, I'm ready," she said.

"Rita, you don't know what you're talking," Rick said.

"I do, sweetheart. And you do too. Anytime you want to try, you just give me the word. I love what you got," she said and gave his bulge a gentle squeeze and walked away.

Rick wondered if he should try. It was true he'd never been to bed with a girl. He didn't care for them. But maybe he should find out, maybe he'd never get another chance like the one offered by Rita.

That night after Turk had gone to bed, Rick left the TV on, not too loudly, so that in case Turk woke up he'd know that Rick was still watching, and went out. He knew where Rita stayed, at the far end of the beach in a cooperative apartment unit.

Wearing his red speedos and a white sweat shirt, Rick walked barefoot on the sand to Rita's place.

Rita opened the door. "Why didn't you tell me? I was just going out to a late movie with Van."

"That's okay, Rita, I'll see you another time," said Rick, almost glad to have an excuse to get away. He was turned off by Rita's heavy perfume.

"Oh, no. You're not going to get away that easily. Come on in. I can go to a movie with Van anytime. You're top meat, hard to get you," she said, literally dragging Rick inside the apartment and closing the door. She called up Van and cancelled her movie date.

"That's taken care of. See how easy that was? Like a drink?" she asked.

"No."

"Like some music? Want to dance?"

"No," said Rick feeling awkward.

"Okay, then," Rita said, coming close to Rick and hugging him. "Would you like one of Rita's special knee trembler blow jobs?" she asked cupping his crotch.

Rick embraced her furiously and kissed her, to arouse himself.

"Wow, take it easy," said Rita, taken by surprise. But when she tried to kiss him again, gently, he turned away his face.

Rita walked away and put a record on the player.

"You know what this is?" she asked.

"Sure. Ravel's 'Bolero'."

"Good. And it always turns me on," Rita said and started to do a strip. "Come on, Rick, off with your sweat shirt, then off with your speedos," she said.

Rick wanted to leave, but decided to go through with it. He started to undress. Looking at his thick meat tumble out of his tight speedos, Rita got very excited. Swinging her body in rhythmic movement, she came close to him, but Rick was repelled by what he saw: the swinging breasts and the flabby buttocks. When Rita embraced him and started caressing his cock, Rick shrank back. Rita became aggressive, pushed him on to the couch and started to paw over him, kissing him and uttering words, wild, exciting, reckless words to arouse him. She squeezed Rick's cock, and licked his balls, but Rick stayed limp. "Sorry, Rita. It doesn't work," he said, pulled himself away and stood up. He quickly eased back into his speedos and sweat shirt.

"I'm sorry, Rita. I really am," he said very apologetically.

"That's okay, kid. I tried to help," Rita said. She got up and reached for the phone and dialed and said, "Van, baby. Huh? Listen, my plans changed again. Can you come on over, right now? I'm all moist and wet, ready for you. Hurry over. Okay?" and hung up.

"Rita, please keep this to ourselves. Please," Rick said.

"Of course, sweetheart. This world is big enough for all kinds and all forms of love. Take care," she said and kissed Rick on the cheek.

Rick came out. The female form definitely did not turn him on. Well, that's that, he decided. He returned to the apartment and wanted to wake up Turk and make love to him. He decided otherwise. Instead he got into bed and, thinking of blond Otto, jacked himself off to sleep.

Next day he met Rita, who spoke to him as usual, helped with things, and made no reference to what happened the night before. He liked her for being a good sport. Otto looked particularly attractive in his tight skimpy flesh toned bikini and his short sexy haircut. Rick created an opportunity to pat Otto's buns and say, "Hey, Otto, you look terrific today."

"You're not-bad-looking yourself, stud," Otto said and patted Rick's ass in return. Rick wondered if he could make the scene with Otto someday. He certainly was turned on by Otto's round behind.

In the gym, Rick kept to himself, making no contact with any of the other body builders, except casual limited conversation. Several guys tried to strike up a friendship with him, but Rick remained arrogantly aloof. There was however one guy with whom Rick talked a little more than he did with others. His name was Mike Snow. Mike was in his mid thirties, probably, but maintained a trim tight athletic figure. He came regularly to the gym, but just did a few abdominal excercises, used the pool and the steam room and left. He struck up a friendship with Rick, and once gave him a ride in his luxuriously upholstered red-and-white Thunderbird. Mike also reminded Rick of his highschool basketball hero Jim O'Neal. Mike made no passes at Rick, unlike the others who, within a few minutes after they had started talking with Rick, wanted to either suck him or get fucked. Rick liked Mike for his pleasant talk and good manners, and for not asking all kinds of questions like where he lived and what he did.

As the months passed, Rick's whole personality underwent a change. His eyes regained their deep, dark, brooding good looks as a result of good food, rest and freedom from tension. One day after a vigorous sweat-streaming workout, Rick took a steam bath and a soapy shower, and standing in front of the full length mirror in the shower room, rubbed his body vigorously till it gained that warm healthy glow. Rick liked what he saw, and found it hard to believe in the transformation. The shoulders had broadened with rounded deltoids, the chest had expanded with the pectorals shapely and massively thrust out and the brown nipples tough and taut. The torso was V shaped, the thighs muscular and chiseled, and the broad back tapered into well-shaped round butch buttocks. Rick noticed that while he watched his reflection in the mirror, many were sneaking looks at him. He felt proud and confident once again. He arrogantly ignored the gym spectators and saying to himself, drool, you cocksuckers, drool over me, he withdrew into the dressing room and pulled on his pants and shirt and came out.

"Turk, I caught a good full-length image of myself in the mirror, and Turk, you should see the fantastic development. You see . . ."

"Please, Rick, don't describe yourself to me and torture me. All I have to do is to control myself for another sixteen days," said Turk.

"You mean in just sixteen days it'll be a year since I've been with you?" asked Rick. "I'm ready to bust loose on the sixteenth day and show off?"

"Yes. I'm dying to see your imprisoned splendor bust loose," said Turk.

"You sure you don't want a sneak prevue today?"

"You're the devil when it's tempting people."

"I was just kidding, Turk. I want you to put on a big celebration for my unveiling. I love you, Turk, baby. I really do. You've been good to me," said Rick.

"That's the nicest thing you could have said. I love you too, Rick," said Turk.

15

A FEW DAYS LATER, as Rick came out of the gym, it was driz-
zling, and he waited in front of a shop next to the gym. Usually
he would go and work out in the morning, but that day he had gone
in the evening. Evenings were more crowded at the gym, and Rick
just felt that he should parade himself in front of a larger group of
people. It was the streak of exhibitionism in him. He felt happy and
excited at the silent homage he had received in the gym, for as he
worked out in his white bikini, many eager, desiring eyes had
watched him. It was also the first time he had worked out in a bikini,
for Turk had always insisted that Rick work out fully clad in a sweat
suit. But after seeing his full reflection in the mirror, which self-
hypnotized him, Rick wanted to show off his young ripe perfect
body.

The lights had come on in the streets, and Rick stood confident in
his tight white levis and black T-shirt.

"Hello, handsome, want a ride?"

Rick looked and saw that it was Mike Snow in his red-and-white
Thunderbird.

"Hi," said Rick, running from the shop and getting in.

The car moved on.

"How come you're working out in the evening, today?" Mike
asked.

"I was a bit late getting started this morning. Stayed up late watching old movies on TV," said Rick. "Come to think of it, I haven't
seen you at the gym for some time."

"I was away in Hawaii. Just got back yesterday."

"Had a good time?"

"Sure. Ever been in Honolulu?"

"No."

"Nice, although downtown near the Waikiki beach it's like a glorified Coney Island. Have you seen Coney Island?"

"Of course. Used to live in New York City."

"Oh, you're from the big city?"

"Not really. Actually I'm from the midwest, Iowa."

"Iowa? I was born in Iowa. Lived there till I was twenty."

"Where?"

"I was born in Burlington. Then the family moved to Des Moines."

"Really?"

"Yes. And you?"

"Clinton."

"An aunt of mine stayed in Clinton. There are a lot of Iowans in California. In fact, every year they have an Iowa picnic. Ever been to one?"

"No."

"Neither have I. Don't think I've missed much. By the way, I suppose you want to get to Santa Monica. You still live there by the beach?"

"Yes."

"Do you have to be home by a certain time? Study, something like that?"

"Nothing like that, Mike."

"How about having a bite with me?"

"Sounds good."

They drove on and stopped at a drive-in. Rick ordered a sea food salad and a large glass of milk. Mike had two chili burgers.

"What kind of work do you do, Mike?" Rick asked.

"You might say I'm in the entertainment business," said Mike very slowly. Then abruptly, he asked, "Rick, you are gay, aren't you?"

Rick was taken aback by this sudden, direct question. He stammered for an answer.

"Nothing to be ashamed of," said Mike.

"Don't tell me you've done all this to get me to drop my pants?"

"What? You mean buy you this dinner? No, nothing like that. Let me ask you directly, want to make some money?"

"Who doesn't? But then, Mike, I'm through with the hustling bit, making a few dollars," said Rick.

"I'm not speaking of hustling in the street corners and parks. I mean do things in style, make good money, even end up getting a good plush job," said Mike.

"Be more direct, Mike."

"Good suggestion. You see I 'manage' eight superb boys. Good looking studs, healthy, cultured, clean cut looks. One of them is leaving, found a permanent position. I need a replacement. I like to have eight on tab. I have a lot of rich clients, business men, movie producers, actors, you know. Discreetly they make arrangements for humpy young men to service them. I send the right one to suit their individual tastes. I've had my eyes on you for quite some time. Sometimes they . . ."

"You know, I've heard this kind of talk many many times," Rick interrupted with a touch of anger.

"What kind of talk?"

"Your kind of talk. You at least have a nice car, but the others who gave me this line of bull shit, they didn't have a pot to piss in, but they all sold me this big dream. I know this big shot, I know this Hollywood producer, all that bull shit. So I believed them. What happened? They screwed me right and left, promising me a contact, and then kicked me out. Mike, you ought to give your sales pitch to some fresh new kid who ends up here broke and hungry and will go for this bull shit. Sorry, I've listened to this garbage about making big bucks and the big time by getting your ass fucked," said Rick.

"I'm sorry you've had a rough time. But you should hear me out, before you accuse me."

"I can tell you the ending. I don't have to hear it. You'll sweet-talk me, then you'll take me up to your place, and then you'll suck my dick or want to fuck my tight ass. Isn't that what's going to happen? If you like me, say so. Offer me a price. If I agree, we'll go and I'll strip. At least be honest. Please don't give me all this . . . oh, hell," Rick said, getting worked up into anger.

"No, Rick, I don't want you to go to bed with me. I'm not going to take you to my place. All I wanted to know was if you'd be interested in making as much as a hundred dollars on a call."

Noticing that Rick remained silent, Mike continued. "Let's suppose that some business guy from New York gets into town. A buddy of mine in New York gives him my number, like I give his number to someone who wants to have fun in New York. So the businessman who comes here doesn't call me and say, 'I need a boy.' He calls me and says that he's having a party, and asks for a bottle of champagne. I ask him if he needs just one bottle. If he says yes, then I know he wants a guy for a couple of hours; but if he says it's a long party, I know it's an all-night affair. Then I ask him the time and place to deliver the champagne. Then he asks me what kind I got. I tell him I have foreign about 1923. It means a blond boy, aged around twenty three years—you see the last two digits suggest age; that I also have a domestic, which means a dark-haired kid; and native, which means a Black guy. He takes his pick. I tell the selected boy where to go. The kid goes, calls on the man. After the entertainment he collects the money, both his share and mine, he keeps his and gives me mine. So you see it's all carefully worked out, and besides, even if you agree, you are not going to be sent out immediately. The right man has to come. Some of my boys have made permanent contacts, some have ended up as houseboys to some big shots, not that they do much work; they really live a good life. But that I don't promise. All I promise is money on the nights they go out," said Mike.

"Who are the other boys?" Rick asked.

"That's a secret. No boy knows who my other boys are. If you agree to serve champagne," Mike said and laughed to break the tension, "it's between you and me and the guy you serve."

"I'll be frank, Mike," said Rick. "I've always had, and still do, the desire to end up in Hollywood—not just a kept boy of some big actor or producer, but as an actor. But I've been burnt before and have no intention of getting hurt again," said Rick.

"There's no chance to get hurt here. You don't move in with this guy unless you like him, and that doesn't happen immediately. As I said, when I get a call, and if I find that the caller wants someone of your type, then I get in touch with you. You still stay in your place, do what you are doing. But by becoming one of my boys, you just open up more opportunities for yourself. I don't select any boy, Rick. As you can see it's only after nearly a year of watching you that I made the move to chat with you. And that because one of my boys left me. But if you decline, no hard feelings."

There was a pause.

"I guess we better go," said Rick.

They drove back in silence towards Santa Monica, and when they reached the beach area, Rick asked to be let out.

"Sure," said Mike and stopped.

"Mike, thanks for the dinner and the talk. Any place I can call you tomorrow?" Rick asked.

"Of course, here," Mike said and gave him a card with his name and number. "Call me before nine in the morning, or after eleven at night."

"Thanks."

"Rick, take it easy. Give it some thought."

"I will," said Rick and headed towards the beach to think things out.

16

N EXT DAY, RICK CALLED MIKE around 11:30 at night from a pay phone on the beach.

"I think I will deliver some champagne," said Rick.

"I'm delighted, Rick. I am. Give me your phone number."

"You see I stay with another guy. So . . ."

"I understand. I tell you what, why don't you check with me on a daily basis, between three and three-thirty in the afternoon? Is that okay?"

"Yes. But if anything comes up you can call me at the gym and sort of page me. You know that they do that all the time at the gym."

"I'd rather not do that, Rick. All champagne talk we better do the way I've set it out. Call me tomorrow."

"Same number?"

"Yes."

Rick kept calling Mike every day at the prescribed time, but Mike had no champagne delivery for him.

He continued to work out at the gym and kept his conversation with Mike to himself. Turk kept counting the number of days remaining for Muscleboy Ricky's Private Striptease, as he called it.

About a week later, on an afternoon, when Rick called, Mike had a champagne delivery for him. He gave Rick the name of the hotel, the time and directions and asked Rick to take a cab. "I'll reimburse you for it. Then call me after you deliver the champagne, and give me a full report about how everything worked out. This is a very gentle and generous guy," he said.

But Rick did not have any money for the cab. Since staying with Turk, Rick had never worried about money. He used to take about ten dollars from Turk at the beginning of the month, and that was it. His needs had all been taken care of. Food, room, movies, and most of the time he was in a sweat suit or a bikini so that there was no problem of clothes. But Rick now needed at least ten dollars to get to the hotel.

He called up Turk at the music store.

"Anything wrong?" Turk asked anxiously, for Rick had never called him at work.

"No, nothing's wrong. But I need ten bucks."

"Of course. I'll give it to you this evening."

"That's the problem. I need it right now. It's for something like a surprise. Please don't ask."

"Can you get over here?"

"Well . . . yes."

"Wait a minute, Rick. Why don't you borrow from one of your buddies on the beach? Or go to the Tog Shop around the corner from where we are and borrow from Matthew?"

"But Turk, I can't borrow from strangers."

"I tell you what, I'll call Matthew, okay? You go and he'll loan you ten bucks. Is that enough or you want more?"

"That's enough. Thanks."

Rick borrowed the money and then he got dressed and went to get a cab. He arrived at the hotel fifteen minutes earlier than the appointment time, asked the cab driver to let him off a few yards away from the imposing hotel, paid him six-and-a-half dollars, which included a generous tip, and entered the hotel grounds.

It was a plush hotel, judging from the expensive cars in the front. Rick called the room number from a house phone and was asked to come up.

The door opened, showing a very dignified man, completely bald, with a big paunch, wearing expensive dark slacks with red suspenders and a well tailored blue and white striped shirt.

"Good afternoon," said Rick with a very pleasant smile. "I'm Rick, the champagne delivery boy."

The man welcomed him warmly and shut the door after Rick entered.

"Well, well, Mike's boys are getting better all the time. Sit down, sit down," the man added, as he slipped off the suspenders from his shoulders, taking off his pants and hanging them carefully on a chair. "What's your name?" he asked, taking his shirt off.

"Rick."

The man was now in his candy striped boxer shorts. "You won't believe it, but I once played tight end for my varsity," he said and sat next to Rick on the couch. He took Rick's hand and said, "Want to play with me?" and directed his hand to the opening of his boxer shorts.

"Maybe I should get undressed," said Rick diplomatically releasing himself from the rather unpleasant task of playing with the old man's limp cock.

"Yeah, let's see what you got, Rick. I bet it'll put a horse to shame," said the man leaning back on the couch.

Rick undressed slowly and teasingly, and when he slipped off his jockstrap and tossed it at the man, the old man sniffed it.

"Why you're a young, redblooded, healthy stallion," the man said, full of deep-eyed wonder, as Rick strutted naked before him. Closing his eyes and thinking of blond Otto, Rick massaged his cock to a glorious erection.

The old man got very excited and he got on the floor and crawled to Rick like a dog. Rick stood proudly with his legs apart, and the old man sucked him hungrily, gagging on Rick's humoungous equipment. With contempt and pride Rick fucked the man's mouth savagely, but the man enjoyed this aggressive assault. When Rick came spurting all over the man's face and body, there was a look of ecstasy on his face.

Rick showered and dressed and told the man that no one had sucked him so well.

"Really?" the old man asked excitedly.

Rick nodded.

"Wish I had more time. Tell Mike to send you next time I need some action," the old man said and reached for his wallet. He gave Rick a hundred dollars and adding thirty more said, "Give the thirty to Mike. I had promised to give you eighty. But I added twenty as a tip. Okay?"

"Thank you, Sir. Thank you. You are most generous," Rick said.

"Good luck, Rick. Take good care of that great cock you got," the old man said shaking Rick's hand.

It was only five forty-five when he came out. Gosh, that was fast, and good money too, he thought and walked towards a public phone booth on the street.

"When can I give you the champagne money?" he asked Mike.

"Tomorrow afternoon. I'll see you at the beach."

"You know where I lie around. You see, near . . ."

"I know, Rick, I know. See you," Mike said cutting him off.

A couple of days later there was another champagne delivery

arranged, but Mike asked Rick to call him back after he got dressed, for he would drive him. But when Rick called again, he said, "I'm sorry, Rick. There's no party tonight. The guy had some scenes to shoot. Call tomorrow," said Mike, and hung up.

Rick was intrigued by the sentence, "The guy had some scenes to shoot." What did Mike mean? Was this guy a big producer or actor or director. He was very tempted to call Mike and find out, but did not want to upset Mike. All day and night he thought about it, hoping that it'd be a power from the movie world, and that he'd get his big break. He called the next day, but Mike was brief again and said, "Nothing today. Try tomorrow."

He spent another day in suspense, and called the following day at the usual time.

"Okay, Rick. The party's set for next Saturday night. He wants the champagne at seven in the evening. It's a little complicated to get there, so I'll drive you. Be at the gym, out front, on the dot, seven."

"Sure . . ."

But Mike had hung up before Rick could ask him whether the guy he was meeting was the same fellow "who had some scenes to shoot." Well, he'd find out in another four days, he thought, and walked back to the beach. Suddenly a half hour later it struck him, as he was lying on the beach, that the day he had to deliver the champagne was the day he had to do the strip tease for Turk. It would be the twenty-first of March, and Turk was planning the event with great care and eager anticipation.

Of course he couldn't back out now. He had to deliver the champagne, for after all it might be a big guy in the movie world. He also did not want to disappoint Turk. He liked Turk, and after all, thought Rick, flexing his muscles and squeezing his pectorals, this stupendous transformation was due to Turk. He'd have to do his best and manage both. Maybe the champagne delivery would be a short one.

That evening when he had dinner with Turk, Rick was glad to hear Turk say that on the twenty-first, he probably wouldn't be back until eight-thirty or nine. "I can't get away earlier, for my store had some kind of teenage record contest. I have to stick around, but I've already said that I won't be in the following day, so we can have a late night!"

"That's okay, Turk. I'll release my imprisoned splendor at nine when you get back. I'll be all hot and ready for you. I'll even shave my big balls."

"Shave your balls?"

"Yeah. It's real cool and sexy. There's this one blond kid on the beach, named Otto, and he shaves his balls and sort of trims the hair around his crotch. Real sexy. You wait till you see. It'll drive you nuts," said Rick.

"I can hardly wait," said Turk.

Both Rick and Turk awaited the twenty-first eagerly, but both for a different reason. Little did both know at that time that the twenty-first would be a turning point in their lives.

Turk had left by the time Rick got up on the morning of the twenty-first. Rick ate a hearty breakfast as usual, and got out and got a nice trim sexy haircut. He returned and using a hand-held mirror, carefully trimmed his crotch hair and then applied some depilatory cream and shaved smooth his balls. He showered and then gently massaged his big balls with a light cream, wiggled into a white and blue bikini, eased into his levis and headed for the beach.

Time seemed to pass very slowly that day. He returned to the apartment around two, fixed himself a sandwich and a glass of milk, and lay on the bed. Soon he was asleep.

He woke up with a start, cursing himself for having slept so late. It was six ten. He took a shower, admired himself in front of the mirror, put on a black colored jockstrap, a red knit shirt and a pair of tight faded levis, sneakers and hastened to the gym.

Mike picked him up promptly at seven and they drove.

"You look very healthy, hung and handsome. I like your casual outfit," Mike complimented Rick.

"Thanks, Mike. Who's the guy? Any special hints you want to give me?"

"It's Tom Shane."

"The actor?"

"The very same."

"You're kidding," said Rick excited.

"No, I'm not kidding. You'll soon see for yourself."

"But God, he's married, has a wife. I've seen pictures of them all very lovey-dovey."

"Oh, sure. That's for the public. Of course, once in a while, somebody does announce that Tom's gay, but then that's publicity too. But he's crazy for boys like you. Judy, his wife, is crazy for girls. So you see it's an ideal relationship. Both get what they want, and their marriage is a perfect cover."

"That's hard to believe."

"It's the truth."

"I've seen all his movies and he's so very macho in all his pictures."

"One thing you got to remember, Rick. Don't talk too much."

"About what?"

"About your wanting to be a movie star and all that. Tom's a very jealous person, and he doesn't like anyone to compete with him, particularly someone young and hung like you. So hold your horses. Okay?"

"Of course, Mike. How far is it anyway?" Rick asked.

"We'll be there in about another half an hour."

"Where is this hotel, home, whatever?"

"It's Tom's hideaway in the desert."

"In the desert?"

"Sure."

"I thought we'd get back in a couple of hours."

"Oh, no. This is an all-night affair. Very leisurely. You'll like his place, and you'll like Tom too," Mike said and noticing the worry over Rick's face, said, "Worried you did not bring any pajamas? Forget it . . ." Mike laughed.

Rick smiled, but he was thinking how disappointed Turk would be.

It was close to eight thirty when they arrived at the large ranch-style house which was Tom Shane's desert hideaway.

It had been a rough day, but Turk was glad to be out on the road, driving towards his apartment. Anyway, he had now taken leave for a week from Monday, instead of just taking off Friday as he had originally planned. That was a very relaxing thought. He would spend all the time with Rick, go to the beach, make passionate love to his very own Adonis, go out for dinners, and all the fun things. Ah, Rick would be wanting to show off his gorgeous body as soon as he reached the apartment.

Turk did not find Rick in the apartment. At first he was disappointed, but then he decided he was pleased: he would use the time to prepare for the pleasures of the night.

Slowly, luxuriously, he showered, soaping the most intimate parts of his body with a lush lather. After he rinsed and dried himself, he sprinkled perfume lavishly all over his naked body. Then he did something he always wanted to do but never dared: he used mascara on his eyes, then lipstick on his lips. Finally he put on sheer black nylon panties.

He went to the bed and lay back, his legs spread apart, his knees slightly raised. Half-awake, half-asleep, he daydreamed about Rick's forthcoming appearance. He hoped Rick would come from the beach all sweaty and hot and sticky. Slowly he would remove Rick's sweat shirt and pants. As he eased Rick's skin-tight bikini down from his muscular waist he would caress Rick's regal cock, awaken it to its full length, coax it with his tongue till the velvet knob throbbed. Then he would turn over, pull a pillow beneath his crotch and wait for Rick to mount him like a stallion in heat.

"Oh, Rick, Rick, Rick, where are you, my love? Where are you?" Turk moaned and writhed on the bed like a bitch in heat.

They parked the car in the garage, next to another car, and Rick and Mike were greeted at the main door by a balding, but suave looking Black man.

"Hello, Eddie, how are you?" Mike greeted the Black shaking his hand.

"Fine, Mr. Snow. Just fine. I see you've brought a young friend."

"Yes. This is Rick. And Rick, this is Eddie."

They shook hands. "The boss is not in, but he'll be back soon. Can I get you something?" Eddie asked.

"Make me one of your excellent very dry martinis," said Mike.

"Rick, what'll you have?" Eddie asked.

"Just a seven-up," said Rick.

Eddie retired to get them the drinks, and Mike and Rick sat down in the large living room. Mike picked up a copy of *Variety* from the table, and started looking at it. Rick was busy taking in the luxuriously furnished room.

"Is Eddie like a butler?" Rick asked.

"Eddie is everything to Tom: his butler, valet, confidant, and sometimes even a father. You treat Eddie with a lot of respect. He's a superb human being," Mike said.

Eddie brought the drinks.

"Well, Eddie, how's the boss feeling?" Mike asked.

"Fine, but he's working hard. He has to take it easy, that's what I keep telling him. Three films in six months; that's a lot of acting. He sure don't need the money that bad. Yes, he has to slow down. He just completed this last film yesterday, and I tell him to go off on a vacation, relax, and not make another picture for another year or so—you know, till something really good comes along. But who do you think was here just this morning?"

"Mr. Vulture, I suppose," said Mike.

"Who else? And with an armful of scripts."

"Eddie and I call Tom's agent 'Mr. Vulture,'" explained Mike to Rick.

Rick smiled faintly, but got up, for he was the first to see Tom Shane enter the living room by the back door.

Tom looked much slimmer than he did in his movies, and Rick was surprised to see that his hairline was receding and that his temples were gray. Tom concealed these signs of age in his movies. He was in a sport shirt and light tan golf slacks.

"Have I kept you waiting?" he asked, shaking hands with Mike, but looking at Rick.

"It's a pleasure to wait for you, Tom," said Mike and shook hands.

"And you are Rick?" Tom asked, giving his hand to Rick.

"Yes, Sir," said Rick, trembling with excitement.

"Sir? Ah, I like that, even though that might make me feel old. Sit down, sit down," said Tom, putting his hands on Rick's shoulders. "Eddie, you think you can fix me a good tall glass of iced tea with plenty of fresh lemon?"

"Certainly," said Eddie and left the room.

"I understand the film's completed," said Mike.

"As far as I am concerned," said Tom, his hands still on Rick's shoulders.

"So now you'll follow Eddie's advice and get some rest?" Mike asked.

"Eddie worries too much. But then I know he cares for me. You know, it's been twenty-nine, no, thirty years, since Eddie's been with me. Since I was nineteen. Well, I've told my age now. I feel so old when I see someone so young like Rick," he said, squeezing Rick's shoulders.

Eddie brought in the iced tea.

"Thanks, Eddie. You know, I was planning to see an old movie of mine, one that I made in Rome, around six or seven years ago. It's never been released, but they are planning to. My agent thinks that a nationwide multiple release of movies in which I've starred, one after another, would be good. You know—go to any movie, Tom Shane's sure to be in it. But frankly, after I made *Roman Nights*—that's what it's called—I never saw it. It's one of those super colossal costume affairs. Want to see it?" he asked.

"Sure," said Rick with great excitement.

"I can stay," said Mike. "But it depends on Rick, I mean, if I have to take him back to L.A. tomorrow, I better stay and drive him. But if you want him to stay tomorrow as well, then I'll leave and come back Monday," explained Mike.

"It's late, why don't you stay, Mike? We'll have dinner and watch the movie. You can give me your critique as well," Tom said. "Eddie, is the movie room all set up?"

"Oh, yes."

"Let's go. Eddie, let Mike take the blue room. That's comfortable."

"They all moved to the movie room which was in the basement, furnished like a mini moviehouse, with very comfortable chairs and a big couch in the front of the large screen. Very discreetly, Mike went and sat on a chair on the back, while Tom and Rick sat on the couch.

Eddie brought in some trays with sandwiches. Tom declined, just asking for his iced tea to be refilled. Rick helped himself to the sandwiches. They were good. After Tom had his iced tea refilled, all the lights were turned off. Eddie began the film.

Tom took a few sips of iced tea, kept it on the side, and dragged Rick closer to him. He put his arms around him and they started watching the movie.

There was no sign of Rick, and Turk moved restlessly in his apartment. He put on some records, and saw Rick's tan bikini in the bedroom. Turk picked it up and sniffed it. Turk held it tenderly, pressed it to his chest, then put it on the pillow, "Rick, Rick, where are you?" he moaned softly. He fondled the bikini and kept kissing it.

He lay on the bed gazing at the ceiling for some minutes. "To hell with you, Rick. To hell with you!" he shouted at last. Jumping out of bed, he put on a T-shirt and a pair of slacks, slipped into his sandals, quickly removed his lipstick and mascara, washed his face, and left the apartment and got into his car.

He drove fast, furiously and aimlessly for a long while, then abruptly turned onto the road leading to Hollywood Boulevard. While waiting for a traffic light, he noted on a clock on a storefront that it was close to midnight. He had heard of a coffee shop on Hollywood Boulevard where gays were supposed to gather. He headed in that direction, parked his car in an all-night parking lot and went searching for the coffee shop.

He found it with no difficulty, for the shop was crowded with guys, both buyers and sellers.

Turk managed to squeeze into the coffee shop. There was no place to sit, but he was quickly appraised by the crowd. The moment a counter seat got vacant he rushed and occupied it. Next to him was a tall, rangy, cowboy type of a guy, possibly in his early twenties. He had a rugged look about him and Turk glimpsed the big bulge resting on the seat.

"I'm from Cody, that's out in Wyoming. Where you from?" the guy asked Turk.

"Right here."

"So you're a native, an Angelino? You sure look sweet as an angel," the guy said smiling.

Turk was attracted to the guy. "Would you like me to show you around?" Turk asked.

"That's mighty sweet of you," said the guy and stood up.

He reached for his wallet to pay his check, but Turk quickly picked up the check and said, "Let me."

"You're not only sweet but generous. Thank you," the guy said.

They came out and headed toward the parking lot, picked up the car and started driving.

"What's your specialty?" the guy asked.

"I love to get fucked," said Turk.

"I got a big one," the guy said.

"I can take big ones. My lover has a big one. Like a horse," said Turk getting turned on by this frank talk.

"So you have a lover?"

"Yes. A big beautiful muscle boy. Juicy."

"Why aren't you with him now?"

"Well . . . let's just say I wanted a cowboy," Turk said and reached for the guy's crotch.

"Later. Later. Drive carefully," the guy said.

"I can hardly wait, " said Turk.

"You pick up guys to get fucked?"

"Once in a while."

"You pay them?"

"I'll pay you, don't worry."

"How much do you pay?"

"How much do you expect?"

They were now on the Hollywood Freeway.

"Ever hear of the vice squad?" the guy asked.

"Why?"

"Why? Because I'm from the vice squad. See?" The guy lifted himself from the seat, pulled out his wallet and quickly flashed what looked like a badge. "Keep driving to the station. I'll direct you."

Turk froze. Oh, God, what had he done! Turk thought. He couldn't afford to go to the station. Not a scandal. Maybe he had acted hastily in coming away. Maybe Rick was back right now in the apartment waiting for him. Or maybe Rick had had an accident and was in some hospital. Or maybe Rick had planned a surprise for *him*. Turk's mind raced a million miles scripting different scenarios.

"So? What do you say?" the guy asked tauntingly.

"About what?" Turk asked.

"Well, about getting locked up with other criminals and per-verts?" Among the many different scenarios his mind had scripted, there was one where he was not running away, nor retreating to the closet, not being treated like dirt. Earlier he had shouted in the privacy of his apartment, 'To hell with you, Rick. To hell with you.' That mood of defiance quickened his adrenaline. What are you afraid of? he asked himself. He hadn't stolen, he hadn't hurt anyone, all he had done was ask a guy in a gay coffee shop if he wanted to have some fun. He was even prepared to pay for it. He was not forcing anyone. This guy sitting next to him was trying to trap him. To hell with him. Yes, to hell with him, he decided. He wasn't going to be afraid. Maybe he was not even a part of the vice squad. No, don't panic, he told himself. Keep cool. Don't be afraid.

"Cat got your tongue?" the guy asked.

"I'm not afraid," Turk said.

"Ever hear of gang rape?"

"Sounds like a lot of fun," Turk said looking straight ahead, and smiling.

"You some kind of weirdo?"

Turk responded by increasing his speed.

"Hey, take it easy," the guy said.

"I want us to get there before the place closes down."

"What place? What the hell are you talking about?" There was a streak of fear in the guy's voice.

"Don't worry. Keep cool."

"Why the hell should I worry? You're the one who's the queer."

"You tell *that* to my buddies."

"Your buddies?"

"My protectors. Six of them, big strong muscleboys. That's

right, mister. I run a big stable of hunks. They hate vice cops. They'll tear you limb from limb, giving you a taste of that gang rape you talked about," Turk said, confident and in full control.

"Hey, take it easy," the guy said, because Turk had increased the speed.

"I am taking it easy."

"Hey, listen. I was just kidding. I'm *not* a vice cop. See this badge . . ."

"Just shut up. Shut up, you son of a bitch," Turk shouted at the top of his voice and pulled over to a side bringing his car to a screeching halt.

"Go on, get out. Go on, before I change my mind," Turk ordered. The man literally tumbled out of the car.

Turk breathed a sigh of relief, started to laugh and drove back to his apartment.

Roman Nights ended a little after midnight. Tom had sat through it to punish himself. Mike had yawned with no restraint in the back seat, for there was no one to watch him. Rick had a hard time controlling his yawns. *Roman Nights* was a perfect example of how not to make a movie.

Don't turn on the lights, Eddie," said Tom as the movie ended. "Good night, both of you. See you in the morning and then we can tear the movie into bits."

Tom sat still for a few more minutes in the dark with Rick. Then he embraced him and cupping Rick's crotch kissed him passionately. "Let's go and make love," he whispered to Rick after the kiss.

They left the movie room and walked up the stairs to the large bedroom at the end of the corridor.

"Want to take a shower?" Tom asked.

"Yes," said Rick, realizing that Tom wanted him to take one.

Tom showed him the fancy bathroom and said, "I'm going to eat out your sweet ass, so . . ."

"I'll have it clean and smelling fresh," Rick said smiling.

"Good boy," Tom said and left him.

Rick showered, luxuriating in the splendid shower that had all kinds of fancy gadgets to control the flow of water. He couldn't believe that he was in Tom Shane's house, and was soon going to make love to a movie star. Rick lovingly caressed his cock, awakening it to its glorious erection. He wanted to step out of the shower hard and throbbing. He dried himself, and massaged a few drops of

musk oil, from a bottle on the toilet counter, on to his cock. He liked
his healthy, horny, vigorous image in the mirror, and loosely drap-
ing a towel around his waist walked back to the bedroom.

Tom was still in the other bathroom. Rick examined the bedroom. He turned off the main light, and then dimmed the lights over
the bed. The room was bathed in a soft sensuous glow. He turned up
the bed and fluffed the plump pillows. He caressed himself again to
sustain his erection.

"Ah, there you are," said Tom coming out of the bathroom in a
pale blue silk robe.

"The shower was refreshing," Rick said.

"I see that you are ready as well," Tom said.

Rick tantalisingly dropped his towel to the floor. Tom gasped
when he saw Rick's erection. "Beautiful, just beautiful," Tom said
and moved forward, then knelt and started to caress Rick's shaft.

"Suck it," Rick said.

Tom stared at Rick's throbbing cock.

"Come on, suck it. Lick my balls. Suck out my cream," Rick
urged, as he pressed down on Tom's shoulders and rubbed his cock
against Tom's mouth.

Cupping Rick's balls, Tom opened his mouth and started to suck.

Rick closed his eyes and fantasized Otto, the blond. He gripped
Tom's head and started to pump vigorously into Tom's mouth.
Then he urged Tom with his hands to get on the bed. Tom stood up
and hugged Rick, and let his robe slip to the floor.

They moved and fell on the large bed. Never had Rick known that
such passions could be aroused, for Tom was an expert in the art of
lovemaking, and by touching Rick in special ways, in certain places,
he was able to bring to an intense climax all the desires imprisoned in
that body. Rick responded to every touch of Tom like a musical
instrument that sounds the subtlest notes at the touch of a master.
It was a reckless, wild, unashamed, uninhibited clutching at each
other. Tom turned Rick over and pulling a pillow under Rick's
crotch, parted Rick's tight cheeks and started to scoop him out with
his tongue. Rick was aroused to such intensity that he rolled over,
and pushing Tom on the bed, pressed his legs to his chest and
mounted him with a savage thrust. Tom's scream of ecstasy shat-
tered the silence of the room.

In the early hours of the morning, Tom woke up and looked at
Rick sleeping beside him. Rick slept deeply; it was the slumber of
utter sexual exhaustion. Tom wanted to wake him, feel again Rick's

hard muscular body, but he let his desire ebb. Tom felt his age. Cynically he thought of the image he presented on the screen to millions of people; he was the strong virile male whip in those dreams of celluloid. He was the handsome gunman who single-handedly tamed a wild town, jumping on horses, climbing on mountains, leaping from building to building. He was the quintes-sential macho superman. Women swooned in his arms and fan magazines churned out juicy gossip about his bedroom exploits with top named movie queens. Feeling his flab under the thin sheet that covered him, he admired the work of the cameraman, Paul, who photographed Tom like a hero.

Soon he would have to stop playing the Western hero, thought Tom, for the camera can fool only so much. Rick turned over in his sleep. Tom saw now the half-naked body, half a shoulder and half a round buttock. He wondered if he should keep Rick not just for a few days but for keeps. He was tired of calling Mike constantly for fresh supplies. But he also wondered if Rick, like some other hunks he had bedded, had dreams of becoming an actor. Tom could not stand such aspirations. They were self-seekers. He wanted a hand-some hunk who would stay with him, cater to his desires and be content doing that. He decided to test Rick by asking him some questions and find out Rick's deepest ambition. As he gazed at Rick, he also reflected on Eddie's suggestion that he should take a vacation, possibly in Europe.

Rick, Mike and Tom had brunch on the patio by the swimming pool. Although it was a hearty breakfast of fish, two eggs, corn flakes, orange juice, buttered rolls and coffee, Rick felt hungry. Tom saw him pick up the last roll on the table and eat it.

"It is a pleasure to watch you eat, Rick," said Tom. "You eat with such sensuousness."

"It was a splendid breakfast," Rick said.

"Well, I think I better get on the road," said Mike. "You better hustle too, Rick. I know it's so relaxing here, but we have a long ride ahead."

"Sure," Rick said and stood up.

"Mike, let Rick stay for a few days," said Tom. "Is that okay with you?" he asked.

"Of course," Rick said eagerly.

"Sure, Tom," said Mike, surprised by Tom's decision. "I'll come back to get you . . ."

"Mike, don't worry about Rick's transportation. Eddie can get him back to L.A. or if I'm in the mood I might drive him myself," said Tom.

"Don't tell me you're going to put Rick out of circulation? You're the first one he's met,' said Mike.

"All the more reason why he should stay with me. He's okay," Tom said very appreciatively and gripped Rick's thigh. "I have plans for Rick. Yes. He's very attractive, young, strong as a bull. Would you like to get into the movies, Rick?" Tom asked.

"You're kidding," said Rick.

"I'm dead serious," said Tom.

Rick remembered what Mike had told him earlier. "No, I don't want to get in the movies."

"What? Most young men I've met want to get into the movies before they get into me," Tom said and laughed uproariously.

"I'm not most young men. I know I can't act. I have no interest in that field. This life suits me just fine," Rick said very casually.

Tom was impressed with Rick's answer. He had merely tested Rick, and Rick had passed the test.

Mike realized what a shrewd kid Rick was. "Okay, Rick, see you next time, whenever that is," he said and went to his room to collect his things.

"Is the shindig planned for tomorrow evening, Eddie?" Tom asked as Eddie started to clear the table.

"That's right. Tomorrow evening the joint will be jumping," Eddie said and laughed.

"Tomorrow is my wedding anniversary," Tom said very matter-of-factly to Rick. "How long has it been, Eddie?"

"It's the fifteenth anniversary," Eddie said, heading towards the kitchen.

"So for appearances Judy and I have to throw this big party at our home in Laurel Canyon. Lots of people, and of course lots of photographers. I sometimes think we give these parties for the photographers rather than for the guests. They'll take hundreds of pictures, Judy and me cuddling, cutting the big cake, feeding each other pieces of cake, all that shit! But Judy is a good sport, she plays the game. Why not? She needs the image just as much as I do. But she's okay. You treat her with respect, okay?" he said to Rick.

"Yes, Sir."

"Call me Tom, in private. Use "Sir" when there are others around."

"Yes, Tom."

"I like you, Rick. There's some freshness in you. You're not jaded. You're new to this business, aren't you?"

"Certainly, Tom. My only other sex experience was when I was in high school."

"Who was the lucky guy who got to you before I did?"

"My scout master."

"Your scout master?" Tom laughed. "Really? I thought scout masters seduced young boys only in horny stories."

"Oh, no, Tom. They play around," said Rick.

"Well, you must tell me about it later. All the details."

"I'll be glad to."

"Rick, I want you to stay with me, mabye for keeps. Eddie's been on my back asking me to take a vacation . . ."

"Did I hear you say vacation?" Eddie asked, coming back to the patio.

"Yes, Eddie. We'll definitely plan a vacation after the anniversary tomorrow," said Tom.

"I'm included in your vacation?" Rick asked.

"You're the reason for my vacation. Our honeymoon," said Tom. "Eddie, Jeff or Mr. Vulture as you call him, is going to be here later this afternoon. I'm going to discuss some business with him, and tell him not to line up any more movies for me. You drive Rick to Laurel Canyon and get a head start on the party. I'll join you sometime later tonight. Judy'll probably get in tomorrow. Rick, you'll be the house boy during the big party. Okay?"

"Of course."

"Get him a nice all-white outfit. White linen slacks, a bit snug, and a white waiter's jacket in linen. Wear a red bikini under your slacks, I want the outline to show. You'll look terrific with your dark good looks and that superb tan you got. Another thing, if any of the guys make a pass at you, decline politely. Then tell me who made those passes," Tom said.

"Certainly," said Rick.

Tom stood up, divested himself of his terry cloth robe, and dived into the pool.

Rick watched him for a few minutes, wondering whether he should jump in also, but decided not to. He got up and stretched and said to Eddie who was carrying some items to the kitchen, "Here, Eddie, let me give you a hand."

"Thanks, Rick. I sure appreciate that," Eddie said.

After helping Eddie in the kitchen, Rick returned to the patio.

Tom was not swimming. It was warm and the pool looked so inviting. Rick decided to take a swim. He went into the kitchen and asked Eddie if it was okay for him to use the pool. "Of course, Rick. Enjoy," he said.

Rick stripped and dived nude into the pool. He swam for about an hour, felt invigoratingly refreshed. He then came out, dried himself and wrapping the towel around his waist returned to the bedroom. He left his clothes and entered the bathroom to shower. Just before he turned on the shower, he heard voices in the bedroom. It was Tom and Eddie.

"So, what do you think of Rick?" Tom asked Eddie.

"Nice boy. First boy who ever offered to help me in the kitchen. He's so polite, he asked my permission to use the pool," Eddie said.

"I'm glad you said that. I dangled that moviestar business, but he turned it down. He's just a clean cut fresh farm boy," Tom said.

"Do you like him, Tom?" Eddie asked.

"He's splendid in bed. A regular stallion."

"As long as you enjoy what you like. But do take that vacation. I mean it, Tom. With Rick around on that vacation you can unwind," said Eddie.

"But you keep an eye on him, Eddie."

"That I will, that I will," said Eddie.

The phone rang somewhere in the living room. "That must be Jeff," said Tom. "Let me get that, Eddie. Call the phone company from the kitchen phone and see that they fix the phone in this bedroom," said Tom and hurried out.

Rick held his breath until Eddie had left. Rick decided not to take a shower. Instead he tiptoed out of the bathroom and made it back to the poolside. He lay by the side of the pool on his stomach and pretended to sleep.

A little later when Tom came and sat next to him and started massaging and squeezing Rick's buns, Rick woke up and stretched and said, "Oh, it's you! I must have dozed off."

17

RICK PINCHED HIMSELF SEVERAL TIMES to make sure he was not dreaming, for he could hardly believe that it was he walking around with a tray of canapes, offering it to celebrity after celebrity. It was incredible! Looking at the faces of his many movie heroes so close, smiling at them as he offered the tray of snacks, Rick felt exhilarated if anyone picked up a canapé and smiled back at him. They kept coming endlessly, the stream of celebrities, and Rick circulated with enthusiasm and sheer delight in and out of the gathering.

Eddie was in the kitchen and at the bar supervising everything. Tom and Judy put on a superb performance as the very happily married couple. Mimi, the celebrated columnist of "I tell tales, but they are all true" proposed a toast by saying, "If there were even two more marriages as happy as Tom and Judy's, all this talk about Hollywood's moral decline could be avoided. To another century of joyous wedded bliss to Tom and Judy!" the crowd applauded, flash bulbs popped and Tom and Judy hugged each other with passion.

It was a grand affair, and Rick was delighted to be a part of it. He *had* come a long way.

There were seven at the party who made passes at him. He made a note to give a detailed description of these pick-up attempts to Tom, after embellishing them properly. One was a teen-age singing star in butt tight designer jeans and a long sleeved pale blue shirt; a playwright with a paunch and a recent Pulitzer award; a stuntman who had been a former football jock in a pinstripe suit; a balding producer who had bankrolled Tom Shane's latest movie; a young actor who was being touted as the next James Dean; an elderly balding man escorting a Marilyn Monroe look-alike blond and a short skinny guy who called himself Tom's former agent. They all seemed to have the same approach when they made a pass at Rick: I'm giving a party for a big gathering soon, you think you could work for me? You're doing such a splendid job. And then asked where they could reach him, and for his phone number. Rick felt pleased with all this attention. He mentioned it to Eddie who said, "If you know what's good for you, keep away from them. The Master won't like that!"

"I was just reporting to you, Eddie. I'd never leave Mr. Shane," Rick assured him. He politely declined the offers made by others, and that only served to whet their hunger for Rick even more.

The last in the party stumbled out at 4 A.M. and Rick stayed up with Eddie until the early hours of the morning, helping him straighten out things.

"Go get some sleep, kid, after I fix you some breakfast," Eddie said. "You must be dead tired. I am."

"But I liked it. All those fabulous stars," Rick said, with wide-eyed wonder.

"Yes, stars. But after you've seen as many parties as I've seen, it's just another reason to get plastered," said Eddie.

After having some breakfast Rick went to his well-furnished room in the basement. He lay awake for a long time before falling asleep. He had sort of expected Tom to come and maybe give him a blowjob, but Tom did not show up. He decided to play his cards right. He was going to be very nice to Eddie, for Eddie had clout with Tom. Rick was also going to be very nice to Tom, satisfy all his desires and keep his ambition to become a moviestar to himself. He would wait, not rush matters. He was confident the opportunity to realize his dreams would come, and when it did, he'd be ready.

Rick did not see Tom for the next three days. "He and Judy are attending parties in their honor, guests of the movie big shots, you know," explained Eddie. "Poor Mr. Shane, he has to put up with all this. If I were him I'd retire. He's got enough money to last him two lifetimes. He should take it easy. He's not a young man, you know," Eddie added.

"You like Mr. Shane very much, don't you, Eddie?" Rick asked.

"Like he were my own son. I brought him up. His mother, Miss Adelaide, had Mr. Shane out of wedlock. That was in Savannah and during those days that was a big crime. She died and left Mr. Shane in my care. Well, that's a long story. We've gone through some rough times. But he's a fine man, just a fine man. Lot of talent."

"He has a lot of talent," Rick said, feeling he had to say something.

"Yes. But not like he used to have. In this business, you have to quit when you're at the top, if not you're bound to get hurt," said Eddie.

"Why do you say that?" Rick asked, curious to learn as much as he could about Tom and about the movie business.

"Never mind that now. Come on, let's get some work done," said Eddie smiling.

Rick had been showing deference and affection to Eddie these past three days, and that morning he had even served Eddie a hot cup of coffee and his favorite roll in bed. Eddie had warmed up to Rick.

There was a well-equipped gym and a large swimming pool in the big house. Rick checked with Eddie and got his okay to use the facilities. As he again examined his nude body in front of the full length mirror, after a hard workout, with sweat streaming down his sculptured physique, he felt proud. He owed this splendid body to the inspiration and motivation that Turk provided. Turk was really his benefactor. It was because of him he had gone to the gym religiously. It was because he went to the gym that he had met Mike Snow. It was because of Mike Snow that he had Tom Shane and now ensconced himself in these comfortable and prosperous surroundings. Poor Turk, Rick remembered for the first time since he had been away. He wanted to see Turk desperately, get in touch with him at the earliest and explain, and possibly work out a plan where he could be away for a couple of days to satisfy the sexual hunger of Turk. He owed Turk that much at least, at the very least.

He decided to take Eddie into his confidence. "Eddie, I need your help," he started. "I was living with a buddy of mine, sort of sharing an apartment. I need to see him, pick up my few belongings and then get back. How can I do that?"

"Sure thing, Rick. But don't go telling anyone where you're staying and give them a phone number to call and so on. If you do that, you'll have all kinds of calls or even visitors. And *that*, I can tell you, Mr. Shane won't like. Understand?"

"Certainly, Eddie. I will not breathe a word of where I'm staying. I promise. I just want to let this guy know I'm not coming back. I was planning on moving out anyway. I owe him a few dollars; I'll pay and say goodbye. That's it," Rick said.

"Just shut out the outside world while you're here," advised Eddie.

"I sure will, Eddie," he promised and asked Eddie for directions on how he could get to the Santa Monica beach and back. Eddie helpfully showed him a map and even permitted Rick to borrow the station wagon.

Rick drove to Turk's apartment but found that a new lock had been installed. There was also a sign which read: For Rent, Call— with a phone number listed. Rick tried to look inside the apartment, but the windows were closed and the drapes drawn inside. He wondered what could have happened to Turk, where he could have moved to. He noted the phone number and drove over to the Tog Shop to see if Matthew knew the whereabouts of Turk.

Matthew told Rick that Turk had moved out, just a few days ago, probably to San Francisco.

"Did he leave any kind of address or number, or anything?" Rick asked.

Matthew shook his head. "He was quite bitter about you though. I know he was concerned about where you'd gone. He must have checked every hospital, asked all your muscle buddies. But then he gave up. When he came to see me a couple of days ago to say good-bye and ask if he owed me any bills he should take care of, I asked him if he'd heard from you. 'That damn son of a bitch, he's probably getting his ass fucked by some other guy. As far as I'm concerned, Rick's dead to me. If you run into him, tell him that.' That's what he said. Couldn't you have called him, dropped him a note or something?" Matthew asked.

Rick was shocked and tears flooded his eyes. As he slowly kept walking back to the station wagon, he realized how Turk had really been his only friend; how it was only Turk who had tried to build a lasting relationship. He sat in the car and wept for losing Turk, for his own betrayal of a friend who had helped him when he was down and out. He was so enveloped in his grief that he was startled when he felt a hand on his shoulder through the window.

It was blond Otto.

"Hey, Rick, what's the matter? Where have you been? Is everything okay?" Otto asked.

Rick managed to smile and nod his head and wiped his tears.

Otto, who was in his usual outfit, his skimpy fleshtoned bikini, walked to the other side of the car and got in and sat next to Rick. He put his arm around Rick and asked, "Can I help?"

Rick burst into tears again and feeling the need to share his sadness with someone, told Otto of his relationship with Turk, and how he had betrayed Turk by going away. Otto tried to console him, and in the process, they hugged each other, and Otto's hand groped Rick's crotch. "Let's go over to my place. Come on, come on," Otto urged and they drove to Otto's place. They made love and Rick who had yearned for Otto's superb blond body was able to mount Otto. The release of this sexual energy calmed Rick, and he headed for Tom Shane's home in Laurel Canyon. On the way he stopped and bought a packet of Eddie's favorite brand of chewing tobacco as a gift for Eddie.

He told Eddie that his former roommate had just moved out with no message about his whereabouts. "That's okay. All I had were a couple of pairs of Levis and a few bikinis," Rick explained.

"Well, when Mr. Shane returns, I'm sure he'll buy some clothes," Eddie said.

"One doesn't need much clothes in this nice warm weather, anyway," said Rick. "Just a couple of shorts."

Tom and Judy came back on the weekend, and Rick was introduced to Judy as the houseboy. Rick was given the once over by Judy and he was not certain whether she approved of him or not.

On Sunday afternoon, Eddie and Rick drove to the desert house in the station wagon. Tom was supposed to join them the next day.

The following morning, Tom came down late for breakfast. His eyes were bloodshot and he looked weary and haggard. "Hello," he said softly to Rick and sat down. For the next twenty minutes there was an awkward silence while Eddie served breakfast. Tom kept drinking one cup after another of black coffee. Rick felt very uncomfortable and embarrassed, for he did not know what to say or do. Then he hesitantly said, "Tom, you must have been very busy these past few days."

"Yes," Tom replied. "Come join us, Eddie. I better get this off my chest."

Eddie sat down and poured himself a cup of coffee. Then Tom started to speak.

Tom and Judy were being dined and wined by Grant Stenson and his wife, at their home in Balboa, in honor of the wedding anniversary. Then they had decided to go cruising in their yacht for a few hours. The Stenson's maid, a buxom Swiss-German named Anna-Marie, whom they had recently hired away from one of their friends, came along on the cruise. She was a very attractive girl whose English was limited, but who, according to Mrs. Stenson, was a perfect maid. Like many wealthy people, the Stensons discussed nothing but the maid for hours on end, both in their house and on the yacht. Judy had taken a more than usual interest in the discussion, jesting several times with Rose Stenson that she might lure the maid away. Tom suspected that something might happen, an unsightly scene, because Judy had had quite a few drinks. She was hysterically gay on the yacht, and Tom suggested that they return to the shore at once. Tom also knew that Judy had just broken up with Andrea, her girl friend. The Stensons hesitated at first, but complied and returned.

The embarrassing thing that happened that night was what Tom had hoped to avoid. Judy attempted to seduce Anna-Marie, the girl resisted, and Judy lost her temper. There was nothing that Tom could do to soften or whitewash the incident. When Tom tried to reason with her, Judy screamed that he was being selfish. "You have that hot horny hunk, Rick. Let me have mine. Leave me alone," she shouted and slammed the door in his face. Tom had never witnessed such fury on the part of Judy before.

With apologies to the Stensons, Tom had left later with Judy, now calm enough to come with him. They traveled silently, and as they entered Los Angeles, Judy stated very flatly that she was going to leave Tom. She was sick and tired of this charade they had put on for these many years. Where she was going to, or what she was going to do, she said, was no concern of his; but he had to give her a big chunk of his money and property. She knew that her life would be laid bare if Tom went to court, she acknowledged; but if Tom did go to court, she stated bluntly, then she would reveal his secret life. She would even write one of those juicy gossipy books titled "My Life with Tom Shane" and name names. Her irrational vindictiveness saddened Tom, but he knew that she would go ahead with it.

He agreed. Within a few days he promised he would see the lawyer and settle Judy's share.

Tom told Eddie and Rick all this in a very quiet voice, one without hysteria or emotion. Eddie was the first to speak, and he said, "Tom, maybe this is for the better. Now that Judy's leaving you, you're freer than ever before. A man your age can live like a bachelor once again, free of putting on a show. Give her what's coming to her, then forget her. Take a vacation, relax as much as you can. You've been driving yourself too hard. When you come back after some rest, select a script that's really good—maybe do one a year, or at the most two. Even look for some occasional work on TV."

"Well, we'll see. I'll take it one day at a time. But I do need a vacation," said Tom. Then he turned to Rick, smiled, reached out and touched his hand and said, "How's this gorgeous boy doing?"

"He's okay, Tom. He'll work out, just fine. Just fine," said Eddie winking his eye at Rick and smiling.

"Glad to hear that," said Tom looking at Rick.

"Well, I got work to do. You guys sit and chat," said Eddie and quietly left, closing the door behind him.

"Tom, if there's anything I can do, anything at all," Rick said.

Tom smiled and squeezed Rick's hand and said, "You can stand up, drop those shorts and let me suck your thick meat."

Rick smiled and said, "I was wondering when you'd give me pleasure."

"It's the other way, sweetie. You're the one who gives me pleasure," said Tom getting off his chair and kneeling.

Rick moved and stood in front of him.

Tom eased down Rick's gymshorts. "You're always ready, aren't you?" he asked stroking the half erect cock.

"I've missed you, Tom," Rick said feeding his now fully erect cock into Tom's mouth.

18

JUDY DROVE A HARD BARGAIN, claiming more than Tom had expected. She had her lawyer threaten him with the possible publication of her autobiography titled "My Fifteen Years with a Queer." Tom couldn't believe that such a transformation had come over her.

"What happened to you so suddenly, Judy?" he asked.

"Oh, no, don't say 'suddenly' because nothing happens suddenly. It all keeps simmering, boiling and then it explodes," she said.

"But I've always treated you right. Just a few days before this unfortunate Balboa incident, I told Rick how wonderful and cooperative you were. How lucky I was to have you as my . . . companion."

"Yeah, your houseboy. You've got your fucking sex life worked out just the way you want. But I haven't. I can't get a damn girl to beat up. Get my kicks," Judy said.

Tom got a glimpse into the violent, sadistic sex life that Judy wanted, but was unable to get. He trembled inwardly and felt surprised how very little he knew about his well dressed, attractive lady who had posed as his wife these fifteen years. He did not argue any more, for he now knew that Judy was driven by some compulsive force which she herself was incapable of controlling. It was just as well to end this relationship before Judy did something terrible that would entangle Tom in greater scandal.

Like any other movie star in the high income bracket, Tom Shane had to lead the life of the rich and the famous. They had to lead this life for their fans, and Judy lived it up. Her tastes were expensive both in clothes, jewelry and in nubile young girls. Tom had gone along.

Now that Judy had been awarded her settlement, nominally half, but in reality more, Tom felt he had to come to grips with his financial position. It was not an encouraging one. He felt like retiring, but now knew that he couldn't afford that luxury. To live the style he'd been used to, he needed money, and so he decided to reduce his vacation to just a month and get back to work.

Eddie disagreed with him, but Tom was firm. He called Jeff to say that he'd be ready for more acting the moment he had some scripts for him. Jeff immediately suggested a costume affair that was ready to be filmed just outside Rome. A sort of spaghetti Western with Roman emperors, is the way Jeff described it. They needed a name star, an American, and Tom would fit the bill perfectly. Would Tom accept? If he accepted, Jeff argued, there would be two added benefits. By going to Rome Tom could take a vacation after the filming, second, he would save on taxes by being in the movie overseas. The whole thing would be over in two weeks, and Jeff said that he could build into the contract a five week shooting schedule so that Tom could use the three weeks' vacation on the film company's expenses.

Eddie didn't like the sound of it, but Tom vetoed and accepted Jeff's proposal. Eddie agreed to accompany Tom to Rome. Rick noticed that Tom seemed more relaxed now that the decision had been made. After dinner, all three watched television. Rick was perturbed because during the TV watching Tom sat apart from him, not making any gesture to touch or feel him. In fact, Tom had not made love to Rick for quite some time. Furthermore, Tom had made no reference to whether Rick should go along to Rome or not. Rick was again troubled by the future.

"I'm turning in, guys. I'm tired. You can sit and watch all night if you want," said Tom getting up and stretching.

Rick was perturbed that Tom had not asked him to go to bed with him.

"Good night, Tom," said Rick.

"No so fast, young man. You need your beauty sleep. Come on," Tom said and extended his hand.

Rick breathed a sigh of relief.

As Tom kissed Rick full on the lips, and hugged him, and squeezed his balls, Rick gently released himself and asked, hesitantly, "Can I stay here and take care of the house while you and Eddie are gone?"

"You'll take care of me in Rome, every day, after I film that wretched movie. You'll fuck me hard, real hard," Tom said and turned over.

Happy and aroused, Rick gave Tom one of his heavy duty macho fucks.

19

TO THE POPPING OF FLASH BULBS and questions by a few newspaper men, Tom Shane took off from the Los Angeles International Airport by jet to New York. Rick and Eddie had left on an earlier flight. Tom's agent, Jeff, had fixed up all the details involved in getting a passport for Rick.

At New York's John F. Kennedy Airport there were not so many flash bulbs or reporters, but a lady reporter embarrassed Tom by asking him if he were not getting a bit too old for the strapping Western roles he was still playing. "I'm only asking in the interests of dramatic realism, Mr. Shane, nothing personal," she added, amidst snickering laughter. Tom fumbled, but Jeff came to the rescue by saying, "Mr. Shane's new role will be his debut into another dramatic field." "Is Mrs. Shane accompanying you?" was the next question by a reporter who had been coached by Jeff to ask that question. Jeff knew that the news of the marriage split up of Tom and Judy after fifteen years, and particularly three or four days after their wedding anniversary, would hit the headlines and get the necessary publicity for Tom Shane. No one was really *that* interested in Tom Shane going to Rome to make a movie.

"Mrs. Shane and I have parted very amicably," said Tom, and Jeff hustled him off, saying they were late for the plane. Tom was sullen throughout the flight, still bothered by that question about his old age and his stereotype roles.

Eddie and Rick met Tom at the Rome Airport. Wearing a pair of tight white tennis shorts and light blue knit shirt, his dark hair groomed beautifully, Rick was a picture of beauty and poise. The sight of him revived Tom. But as they left the airport, Eddie slipped on a piece of glazed metal and fell awkwardly to the floor. In the hospital it was discovered that he had a break in his hip bone and had to spend the nearly one month stay in Rome in a cast.

The script of "The Emperor" was awful. Whoever wrote it had thrown everything into it, from Nero's madness to spaghetti western elements to galaxy wars from science fiction. Tom hated dressing up in a toga and Roman sandals. The director knew little English and was unimaginative and, to heighten the tensions on the set, there was another actor from America, a guy who played the villain of the movie. As far as Tom was concerned , he became a villain in real life also.

Vince Davalos was a refugee from Muscle Beach, who had been bumming around Italy for the past six years playing grunt-groan roles in low-budget Italian movies. He was to have played the Emperor if Tom Shane had declined, so when he heard that Tom had accepted, Vince developed an immediate hatred for Tom. Vince was a muscular stud who walked with a swagger in butt tight jeans, constantly thrusting out his pecs. He looked at Tom cynically and, since Vince had picked up some Italian, he often joked freely with other Italian actors. He even served as interpreter between the director and Tom in interpreting some of the subtler instructions. Every time Vince laughed or joked, Tom thought it was at his expense, so he became very self-conscious and sensitive on the set. Vince started to give instructions to Tom, which Tom resented.

Eddie was right; he should never have accepted this assignment, thought Tom.

Rick had accompanied Tom once to the studio, and soon became the center of attraction. Vince paid special attention to Rick, and so did the director who even suggested that he could write another small scene where Rick could portray the role of a Roman slave boy. Tom grew edgy and jealous and worried that he might lose Rick to Vince. So Tom instructed Rick not to visit him on the set. Rick obeyed. Since he was a stranger in the big city, and Eddie was incapacitated, Tom suggested that Rick go sightseeing and do some shopping for clothes.

Rick would visit Eddie in the hospital, take him fruits and chocolates, and then go wandering down the Via Veneto, stopping in one of many roadside cafés to sip an espresso, or linger around the Spanish Steps to watch the varied crowd of humanity from young Italian hustlers to American tourists. Then of course he'd shop in the elegant boutiques picking up expensive items.

Young, handsome, tanned, healthy, his gorgeous equipment forming a succulent bulge in his tight fitting jeans, Rick projected a very striking image. Many wondered if he were an Italian or American actor. If anyone spoke to him, he would merely smile and move on, heightening his aura of mystery. He saw quite a few Americans, and by their hungry looks, knew that they would give anything to suck his meaty cock.

The clothes he bought, he always showed to Tom, eagerly seeking his approval. And in the evenings when Tom had returned from the movie set, Rick massaged Tom's body and catered to his sexual needs.

Tom breathed a sigh of relief when, at the end of three weeks, he played the last scene in the movie. Now the painful, depressing experience had come to an end.

He returned to his hotel suite, declining the invitation by the studio crew to join in their celebration at the completion of the picture. He had done his part, kept up his part of the contract, and decided to leave earlier than planned back to Los Angeles. There was no way he could relax in Rome, he would do it in his desert home, he told Eddie. Very casually, Rick suggested that Tom should reconsider and stay for another week. But Tom was adamant. "We'll stay for one more day, Rick," Tom said. "Tonight we'll go night-clubbing, just you and me. Tomorrow we'll do a bit of shopping, and the following day we'll catch a flight to L.A. Nothing like home," Tom said.

Rick dressed in a midnight blue silk suit he had bought, and a blue shirt and a silk paisley tie.

"You look stunning, Rick," Tom said. "God, I love you," he said and hugged him.

They came down to the lobby. As they were leaving the hotel, the clerk at the desk said, "Signor, some newspapers for you."

"What newspapers?" asked Tom, going towards the desk.

The clerk handed him a bundle of papers tied with a string upon which was stuck an envelope. Tom hurriedly opened the envelope and read the brief note which said "Read and enjoy," signed at the bottom, "Vince."

They were American newspapers, five of them, three from Los Angeles, and two from New York. Tom ruffled through them and noted the passages he was supposed to read. They had been marked in red.

"Shall I take them up to your room?" Rick asked. "Well, we can leave them here and pick them up later," he added. "Come on, Tom, let's go."

Tom did not answer, but hurried back to the elevator. "What's wrong?" Rick asked, following him. Tom did not answer, but entered the suite, and shut the door, and said, "How do you like that?" as he read the papers, dropping them on the floor. Rick picked them up.

The first was a passage in the column of David Saputo, the Hollywood-and-Broadway columnist:

> *"If anyone wishes to see how that venerable old actor Tom Shane looked when he was not that old, they can see* Roman Nights, *just released. But take lots of strong black coffee to keep you awake.*

A Los Angeles paper reported:

> *"Conrad Gillespie's big best-seller novel* Sturrock Ward *bought by Milton Studios will have Lash Burns in the title of Sturrock. It is indeed a relief to have young new faces, instead of the old ones playing strapping roles of Western heroes.*
>
> *"By the way, word reaches us that Tom Shane is playing Emperor Tiberius in* Emperor, *somewhat reluctantly. If it is the young Tiberius he is reluctant to play, we sympathize with him.*

Another columnist in Los Angeles said.

> *"There's probably more to it than a mere marital break up in the Tom and Judy separation. Our studios ought to put a stop to such a degradation."*

The other two had been equally sarcastic about Tom.

"I told Jeff not to release *Roman Nights*, and damn it, the guy has done it. You are away for a few weeks, and people are anxious to kill you," said Tom, very quietly and softly.

"I'm sorry, Tom," Rick said.

Tom smiled, and drew Rick close to him and held him for a while. "I think I'll be here alone. You go out, have dinner and some fun and come back," he said.

"Oh, no, I'll stay," said Rick.

"No, Rick, go. I do want to be by myself. There's a lot of thinking to be done. I'll go see Eddie and might even bring him back to the hotel tonight instead of tomorrow afternoon."

"Tom, please remember that I'm with you always," said Rick.

"That's sweet of you," said Tom and kissed Rick's hand.

20

TOM, RICK AND EDDIE FLEW BACK TO L.A. Getting off at the L.A. International Airport they drove directly to the desert home. Tom was grateful that the plane was late and had arrived at one A.M. Next morning Tom called Jeff to come and see him immediately. "When did you get in? Why didn't you call me? I'd have picked you up," said Jeff.

"Jeff, how could you have authorized release of *Roman Nights?*"

"Please, hear me out. I really have no control over release or nonrelease," said Jeff.

"Come on over. I want to talk with you about several important matters."

"In a couple of days. I will. I promise. Right now I'm in the midst of this new deal with Lash Burns. You know he's the hottest property now. He's playing Sturrock."

"So I hear. You had told me that I was going to get that role."

"It wouldn't have fit you, Tom. Listen, you'll be on top again, don't worry. Just be patient. I'll call as soon as I get free. Okay?" Jeff hung up.

Jeff came to see Tom three days later, but Tom knew that he was no longer interested in him. Jeff had used up Tom, sucked him dry as it were, and now he was out for fresh new talents. Tom realized as he sat looking at Jeff, how very important it is not only to have talent, but to use it with care, conserve it. But he, Tom Shane had squandered it, had appeared in hundreds of movies. None had reached the mark of greatness or even come close to it. Now he was already receding into the past, and others were coming up, boys like Lash. He saw Rick come and pour some more coffee and return to the kitchen. Rick's youth and virility made Tom ache all over with nostalgia for his own youth.

". . .That's what I say, Tom," said Jeff, concluding, but Tom had not heard one word.

"I'm sorry, what *did* you say?" Tom asked.

"Wait till the three movies you're in come out, maybe by then I'll be on the lookout for a TV series, featuring, you know, a regular Marshall or something like that," said Jeff, pulling out a fresh cigar from his coat pocket and biting the end.

"I don't know if I can take the rigors of TV, Jeff. What I need is a good role in a good script. It's a laugh, but I'll say it; I have to make a comeback."

"Don't be ridiculous. What do you mean 'comeback'? Why, just a couple of months ago when you and Judy had that party, why, everyone was there, it was like a who's who in Hollywood."

"Jeff, we've been in the business long enough, and you know as well as I do, that when you throw a party, people come not to see you, but to be seen, to get part of the publicity, to tell the world that they are alive, they're in circulation. I didn't know most of them. The columnists came to dig up some gossip; the teenagers came because their agents told them they had to come; others came to strut around, reach others whom they haven't been able to reach on the phone. It's all a big charade. Well. I'm not bitter; I just want to get more realistic. I need help, Jeff. Help," said Tom.

"Tom, I understand. I'll call you if anything comes up," said Jeff and got up to leave.

"I won't hold my breath waiting," Tom said.

Jeft left.

"Thanks for making coffee, Rick," Tom said. Since their return, they'd had a restaurant nearby cater all their meals, since Eddie was still incapacitated.

"Any time, Tom, any time at all," said Rick. "I want to help."

Tom still clung to one small hope, and that was that maybe the three unreleased movies would be hits and that they would save his career. But his hopes were not realized. The movies came out; the critics panned them, and the public hated them. They were bad, even Tom had to admit. What had happened to him? He was slipping, slipping fast. Maybe it was not sudden, maybe it had simmered and simmered and exploded finally.

Tom became intensely depressed. He just sat by the pool, pretending to read, but his mind was far away, trying to put the pieces of his life together. The gloom of the desert house was further increased by

Eddie being still in bed and unable to come down and cheer up Tom or give him good common sense advice. Rick felt imprisoned at times. He exercised regularly, swam for a couple of hours, caught the sun by the pool, watched TV, read a few books. He missed the companionship of his musclebeach buddies, missed Otto. He also needed sexual release. He wanted to go to L.A. He hinted to Tom that it might be good if he could go work out in a gym, or even get the work out equipment that was in Tom's Laurel Canyon home.

"Judy's taken that home, Rick. Everything in it," Tom said. He then called up a gym equipment store in L.A. and had them come over to fix up a complete exercise room for Rick in the desert home.

"Oh, Tom, you shouldn't have gone to all this expense," Rick said.

"Oh, baby, you're all I have left," said Tom and hugged Rick and wept.

A few months passed and in that time *Emperor* was released. As expected, it did nothing for Tom, but Vince Davalos got some good critical notices for having played to perfection the role of a sneaking slimy villain. How ironic, thought Tom; the movie was supposed to boost him but Vince had gotten the spotlight. As though to prove this, both the lady columnists of Hollywood agreed that Vince was an upcoming star and should be attracted back to Hollywood.

Rick suggested that Tom should go out, shake off his gloom, mix with the crowd, and put on an appearance of nonchalance. Eddie concurred.

Tom agreed to try. He called Jeff, telling him to fish out some invites for him to certain select parties, for he was interested in ending his exile.

Jeff agreed, but nearly a month passed without any response from Jeff. "See how they leave you," said Tom, full of emotion.

Rick, while feeling very sorry for Tom, now began to worry about his own future. Here he was, eating and living high off the hog, still handsome and young, but it was like being on an island; no one was there to see him, to admire him, to gratify his sensuality. In fact it had been quite some time since Tom had made love to him, and Rick felt his loins stir with yearnings for a night of passionate, wild sex. He desperately wanted another hunk's hard, warm body, someone humpy like blond Otto. Oh, to pump Otto's blond buns, thought Rick and grew restless. He decided to start looking.

A few days later, Jeff called to tell Tom that a week from that date was the gala premiere of *Sturrock Ward* at the Pantages Theatre in

Hollywood. "I want you to come to that, Tom. After the show I'm having a party, to which I invite you," added Jeff. "What is this? Another publicity gag? Me come to see Lash Burns become a star in a screenplay I wanted to do? Come on, Jeff, don't turn me into a public hardluck case," said Tom.

"Listen, Tom, you wanted me to get you some invites for parties. Well, this is the best I can do. You decide if you want to come or not. The invitation is still open," said Jeff and hung up.

But Rick and Eddie both persuaded Tom to accept the invitation. "You have to start circulating," they argued.

Tom called Jeff to say that he was coming. Jeff said, "Fine. I'll fix up some broad you can escort."

"I don't want any broad," said Tom.

"Who're you coming with?"

"Just myself. Maybe with Rick."

"Who?"

"Rick, my houseboy."

"Now I've heard everything. Tom, who you fuck in your bedroom is your business, but when you come out in public, that's another matter."

"You mean I can't bring Rick?"

"If you want to cut your throat in public, that's your business too. Go ahead, do what you want," said Jeff and hung up.

As the days got closer to the premiere, Tom got more and more nervous. In fact, on the morning of the day when the premiere was set, Tom wanted to back out, but because of pressure from Rick and Eddie, he decided to go through with it.

"I never knew movie stars could be so nervous,' said Rick, putting on his rented tuxedo.

"They are the most nervous people in the world," said Tom. "You look smashing, Rick. Maybe the crowd'll mistake *you* for a star."

"That won't ever happen with you beside me. But thanks anyway," Rick said diplomatically.

The hired limousine with the uniformed chauffeur drove them to the Pantages Theatre. Crowds had gathered, ranging from squealing teenagers to elderly women who could barely stand. Tom was nervous, but Rick was excited.

As the car pulled up, the squat M.C. said, "Who have we here? Mr. Tom Shane out of hiding. How are you Mr. Shane?" he asked. Tom was grateful that the M.C. had at least remembered his name. He said, "Fine, thank you." He waved to the crowd, which screamed out its applause. Tom did not know whether it was for him or for the person in the car that had just pulled up. He went inside the theatre and was ushered next to a fellow he did not recognize. He was very grateful that the lights dimmed the moment he sat down. He wished he had asked Rick to come. The movie started.

"Where would you like to go, sir?" the chauffeur asked Rick, driving on after Tom had stepped out.

"Keep driving, I'll tell you," said Rick.

Just a few minutes before the car was to pull up at the Pantages, Tom had got cold feet and thought maybe it would be wiser not to take Rick with him. So he had asked Rick not to get out of the car, but to stay in it, drive the car to wherever he wanted and be back in about an hour and a half to pick him up. "Please, Rick, please," he had whispered, squeezing Rick's hands. Rick suppressing his deep disappointment had agreed to Tom's request.

"Just keep on going?" the chauffeur asked again.

Rick did not know what to say. He thought of going to see Otto, but decided against it. How about going to a movie, he thought. But he did not have any money.

"Do you have any money on you? I forgot to bring my wallet. As soon as we pick up Mr. Shane I'll return the money," Rick said.

"How much do you want?"

"Five will do. Just keep driving and stop at the first movie house. I'll watch the show until it's time to return."

They were just in time to pick up Tom. The large crowd outside the theatre had slightly thinned, although there were still many waiting to catch a glimpse of their favorite star.

It took some time for the car to move to the front, and eager eyes peered in from the crowd. One girl yelled, "Who's he?" spotting Rick's face in the window. "He's delicious," said her friend. Rick was almost tempted to wave at the girls, but he saw Tom step forward to get in the car. Tom waved to a handsome young couple, and the man said, "See you at Jeff's party."

He was buoyant, as Rick could see. "Thanks to you and Eddie for persuading me to come," he said to Rick.

"Where to now, sir?" questioned the chauffeur as they came to a corner.

"Let's go to Beverly Hills, Canon Drive, but take the longer route. I don't want to go there for another hour yet," said Tom. Turning to Rick, he added, "Everything was okay, much better than

I had expected. Met quite a few of my pals, all were wondering what had happened to me, asked me not to take Judy's leaving seriously. What did you do, Rick?"

"I went to see a movie. I owe the chauffeur five bucks."

"I'll take care of that. I'm very sorry that I had to leave you. I do hope you understand," said Tom.

"I do, Tom. I do."

"You have to do me another favor. I'll only stay for a little while at this party. You'll have to find something to occupy you for that time. Please, I'll make it up to you," said Tom.

"Sure, Tom. No problem. I'll just sit in the car," said Rick, again disappointed that he was unable to get into the party where he could have discreetly made a few contacts.

"I got some very good ideas watching *Sturrock Ward*. Lash was good, very good. But then what a story, what crisp dialogue. Anyone could be good in that kind of script," Tom said, and went on excitedly about how he could really make a comeback with a good script and a good director.

But Rick was just there, agreeing mechanically with Tom. His mind was now involved in finding out how he could cash in on his good looks before he lost them. The way Tom was acting Rick was going to be in the background for a long time. He wanted some fun and kicks. Rome was good, so were those first weeks in Tom's house, but then life in the desert home these past months had been miserable. All that silence and gloom. Maybe things might change with Tom's renewed interest, but then they might not.

They arrived in Beverly Hills. "I shan't be too long," said Tom getting off. "Park at the far end, in the rear. I'll know where you are and so it will be easy to leave," he instructed the chauffeur.

The chauffeur followed instructions. "I'll stretch a bit, take a stroll and smoke and be back," said the chauffeur and left Rick alone in the car.

It was dark where the car had been parked, and judging by the number of cars, there seemed to be quite a crowd at the party. It was probably eleven or eleven thirty, thought Rick. By the time Tom left the party and they drove back to the desert house it would be at least two or two thirty in the morning, Rick figured. He sat still in the car for a few minutes, then got out and slowly walked towards the house, where sounds of animated conversation and laughter indicated that the party was in high gear. The main hall was packed with people, and Rick was tempted to go in. With his well dressed appearance, no one would stop him, he was sure of that. He walked in and wondered what he would tell Tom if he were to run into him. Well, he would think of something. He could always say that there was some big drunken guy who had started to bother him. To avoid any embarrassing scenes he had come in to the party. That sounded like a logical explanation. He adjusted his black bow tie, gently pushed back his hair, ran his tongue over his lips and entered the hall.

There were people all over the place. He recognized all the big stars, and even some of the new upcoming ones. A waiter passed by, looked at Rick, smiled and said, "There's another buffet out by the pool, sir, in the back. It may not be so crowded out there."

"Thank you," said Rick, heading towards the pool.

The poolside was equally crowded. People were chatting and laughing. No one seemed to be helping themselves to the food although they were all crowded near the buffet table. Rick walked towards the table, picked up a plate, and noticed a big Nordic blond hunk with a superb tan at the far end of the table. He felt excited looking at him. He decided to move towards him and explore possibilities for maybe a quickie.

"Well, hello," said someone, putting a hand on his shoulder.

Rick turned around and saw a short, bespectacled crew cut person in his early thirties.

"Hello," Rick replied, unable to place him.

"I see you've become successful," the man said.

Rick was perplexed.

"From houseboy to movie star, or at least a guest at Jeff's."

Rick moved away. The man was rather loud and looked like he had had one too many. Rick did not want to draw any attention. He saw the humpy blond chatting with a pot bellied man.

But Rick felt the hand on his shoulder again.

"Don't you walk away, when I'm talking to you," the man said sternly.

Rick noticed that a few people turned in his direction to see what was happening. "Let's move over there," Rick said softly and directed the man to follow him.

Rick walked towards the car, and he had a feeling that the man was walking behind him. Rick returned to the car and sat in the front seat. At least he was back. I need to be careful, he thought. Tom has given me a place to stay, food, clothes. I better not do something stupid and lose it, he decided.

"Ah, there you are," he heard the voice and saw the man who had talked to him. "Let's sit in the back and talk," the man said, placing his hands high on the inside of Rick's thigh.

Rick removed his hand, and said, "What do you want to talk about?" He really wanted to tell the man to go jump in the pool, but was afraid to create a scene.

"About you. What else?" the man said putting his hand back on Rick's thigh.

Rick did not remove the hand. The man continued. "You look handsomer each time I see you."

"You've seen me before?"

"Oh, come on. I talked to you at Tom's wedding anniversary party. You in your nice white uniform and that red bikini underneath. Ah, I notice everything. Ah, now you remember," the man said, seeing the change in Rick's face.

"I was at the party. But did we talk? I don't remember that part," said Rick.

"I'll buy that. I was one of your secret, silent admirers. You were very well protected by that black guy, Tom's confidant," the man said his hand moving a bit further up towards Rick's crotch.

"Let's just talk. Okay?" Rick said and removed the man's hand.

"How unromantic. Talk is a bore. I want some action. What do you say? Shall we go find a room in Jeff's home and let me suck your young hot meat . . ."

"I'm sorry. You are mistaken. I'm not that type," said Rick.

"Don't tell me you go for cunts."

"I may be gay, but I don't shack up with everyone and anyone."

"I'm not anyone. I'm a playwright. I will soon be a director. In fact I think I could use you in my movie."

"I've heard that line before."

"Heard what?"

"About my getting into the movies and becoming a star. But first I got to take off my pants, right?"

"Right."

"What kind of movie, porno?"

"You got me wrong. My movie is called *Rootless*, and is going to be a showcase for new teen-age talents, new faces. I could use you in that," said the man, again putting his hand on Rick's leg.

Rick saw a tall figure dressed in white approach from a distance. Thinking it might be the chauffeur, he hastily asked the man to leave.

"Why?"

"Please, I'll see you later, I promise."

"See me where? Will you call me?"

"Sure. But please go, now."

"But you don't even know my number."

"Give it to me, then."

"Here," the man said, handing him a card.

"Thanks," said Rick putting the card in his pocket.

"You will call me. Right?"

"I promise."

The man smiled and squeezed Rick's crotch quickly and got out and left.

The chauffeur came and asked, "Has Mr. Shane arrived?"

"Not yet," said Rick.

"You're enjoying yourself?" the chauffeur asked sarcastically.

"I always do," said Rick with equal sarcasm.

He wondered if there was any truth to that man's talk about him being a director and making a movie. Was he really a playwright? Well, he was probably someone, for he had been at Tom's party, and now at Jeff's. Maybe he was a party crasher. Anyway, it never hurt to call him. He would call him but make sure before he dropped his pants, Rick decided.

21

TOM WAS IN A JOYOUS SPIRIT for a few days after the party. He told Eddie and Rick how encouraged he was by the many pleasant comments he had received from guests at the party, and how he had renewed faith in himself. He had even talked with a young dynamic new agent, Dick Darrah. Dick was just starting out and wanted to represent Tom. "I'm leaving Jeff to move with Dick," Tom said.

"I'm really glad you feel this way, Tom. But I warn you again that whatever you do, do it carefully. It does not matter if you don't do another film for another couple of years. But pick and choose something that'll bring out your talents," Eddie advised him.

Tom agreed.

Dick Darrah came over in his Alfa Romeo to visit Tom for the weekend. Dick was suave, well dressed, wore big horn-rim glasses that gave him an intellectual look. He allowed Tom to talk, and said as he left, "If my plans succeed, you'll come back with tremendous impact. But think about what I said," he said and left after saying good bye to Eddie and Rick in a very pleasant manner.

Rick was impressed with Dick Darrah, and although Dick had not spoken to him once during the day and a half he had spent with Tom, except to say thank you and goodbye, Rick had the feeling that Dick had observed him quite closely.

Tom wanted to move closer to Hollywood. That had been Dick Darrah's suggestion. Eddie agreed unwillingly, and Tom called Dick to get him a proper place.

Within a week, the house was ready, not lavish, but very comfortable and tastefully decorated in Japanese style. It was located in Beverly Hills, in a rather secluded area. Tom was impressed with Darrah's efficiency in locating a house in such an exclusive neighborhood so quickly.

Eddie was mending and able to take a few steps slowly. Tom was in an upbeat mood, and Rick now had some opportunities to dress up and do the town. Since Eddie was still not back to his former strength, Rick did the shopping and used the opportunity to drive around a bit. He had even gone up to Muscle Beach to see if Otto could be located. There were new faces and new bodies. Otto, he heard, had gone to New York.

Darrah even got Tom a role in a western that was being filmed in Nevada, but it didn't quite materialize because Tom turned it down on the advice of Eddie. The second western that Darrah had lined up impressed Tom. There was meat in that plot and the director had won an academy award a few years ago. But the leading lady refused to star in a film with Tom, saying, "Oh, no, not with that old hag. Why, he's not even a real man. I refuse to be kissed by an old queer." Unflinchingly, Darrah had reported the statement to Tom and had asked Tom directly if Tom was gay. "What if I am?" Tom had roared back. "There are hundreds in Hollywood."

"True, but I don't want one of my very first clients to be one. Sorry," Darrah had said.

Rick had never seen Tom so angry. It was with great difficulty that Eddie calmed him down. Late that night, Rick heard whisperings in Tom's room, which was right next to his. He slowly tiptoed to the wall and heard Eddie counseling Tom to return to the desert home and take it easy. "I'd even suggest leaving Rick go for a while. He's a very nice boy, but . . ." Rick did not hear the rest, but returned to his bed. He did not sleep for a long time, but kept staring at the ceiling. Tom's fortunes were declining, and Rick saw the handwriting on the wall. He had to act fast. But surely he did not want to return to hustling on the streets. He did not want to deliver champagne for Mike Snow either. He was so close, in a way, to the movie world, his dream world. He felt that if he missed this chance to cash in, he'd miss it for ever.

In the morning, Tom told Rick that they were moving back to the desert house.

"When?" Rick asked.

"In a week or two."

After a few minutes, Rick said, very hesitantly, "Tom, I know things are rough for you. I only hope . . . and . . . pray that they improve. I feel very bad that I can't do anything to help. But I am with you always." Rick felt that he had given his short speech the right amount of choked-up emotion to make it sound sincere.

Tom was visibly moved by it. "Thanks, Rick. Thanks. You being here with me is a great support," he said and reached out to clasp Rick's right hand.

Rick felt better, more secure. It meant that for at least another week they'd be here before retreating into the exile of the desert house. Rick knew that eventually he would have to leave Tom. Tom was in no shape or mood to help him. I have to get into the movies, or find another wealthy and prominent star to work for, Rick thought. Both seemed difficult.

He decided to call the playwright he had met at Jeff's house. He didn't expect much, but decided to give it a try.

He called the number from a public phone booth on Wilshire Boulevard.

"Who is this?"

"The houseboy. Remember?" Rick asked.

"No. I don't remember any houseboy. Who is this? I have no time for games."

Rick's heart sank, but then what could he expect, he said harshly to himself.

"Is this Walt. Walt Catling, the playwright?" Rick again asked.

"This is he."

"You do not know my name. But you've seen me twice, at two parties: once at Mr. Shane's and . . ."

"Why didn't you tell me that before, you handsome houseboy. Where are you?"

"Out on Wilshire."

"What are you doing there?"

"Calling you."

"I thought you lived somewhere out on Wilshire. Anyway, I suppose you want to come and see me."

"Yes, very much. I need a job."

"Oh, sure, handsome, I'll give you a job anytime," he said and laughed.

"I'm afraid we're not on the same wavelength. I'm not thinking of the job you have in mind," said Rick.

There was vigorous laughter at the other end.

Rick held his breath, and said, "Okay, I guess you are busy."

"Hey, wait a minute, don't hang up."

"I don't have much time, Mr. Catling."

"Come over. Let's talk."

"Now?"

"Why not? See you in half an hour."

"Mr. Catling, I can see you this evening, around seven."

"That's even better," said Catling and told Rick how to get to his apartment in Westwood.

Rick dressed to impress Mr. Catling. He put on his white waiter's linen trousers and a red bikini under it. He topped it off with a V-neck pale blue cashmere sweater to show off his chest, and a pair of sandals.

Tom was in the living room, reclining on a couch, reading a book. Rick bent over and kissed him.

"Gosh, you're a knockout. You look terrific. Where you off to?" Tom asked, drawing Rick close to him.

"Nowhere. I'm taking you to a movie and later to one of the best hamburger places in L.A.," said Rick.

"No, dear boy. You go and enjoy yourself," said Tom kissing Rick's hands.

Rick had anticipated that answer. However, he insisted that Tom come with him. "I don't want to go by myself," Rick said and sat down on the couch.

"Listen, you are going out and seeing a movie," Tom insisted in a serious voice. After a few minutes of hesitation, Rick left with a sigh of relief that Tom had not changed his mind.

He called Catling from a pay phone and told him he was on his way. He took the station wagon and drove to Westwood.

It was a smallish apartment, but Rick had never seen such a pile of books and papers as he saw now. The walls were covered with pencil sketches, and modern painting prints, and a couple of bull fighting posters. Catling was glad to see Rick, and warmly embraced him.

"You know how to turn me on, don't you?" Catling said and gave Rick's buns a squeeze. "That red bikini underneath. Oh, you devil," Catling said and hugged Rick and laughed uproariously.

"We'll do all that later," Rick said releasing himself. "Tell me about the movie you're making and what chance I've got of being in it," he said moving away and sitting on a chair.

"I will, I will. Want some java?" Catling asked.

"Sure, I can use a cup."

Catling poured Rick a cup of freshly brewed coffee in a mug and gave it to him.

"Oh, you are handsome. Oh, you are so scrumptious. Come on, Rick, come on, let's see your meat," Catling said.

"First we talk. Then I show. Okay? Tell me," Rick said sipping his coffee.

Catling looked at him, smiled, and sitting across from him on a chair said, "You will go to bed with me, won't you?"

"That depends. Listen, Walt, I did not come here to waste time. You met me, you liked me. You want my hot body. I want something too. I want to get into the movies. So I'm here because you told me you can use a new face. Let's make a deal and you can suck my cock," Rick said.

"Boy, you sure are something else," Catling said.

Rick stared at him for a minute, intently, without batting an eyelash, put the coffee mug down, got up, and peeled to his pubes. Standing nude, he caressed his gorgeous cock till it half rose. "Okay, Walt, have you seen anything this humpy ever? This body will be yours. This cock you can suck. These balls you can lick. But first you get me in the movies before you can touch me," Rick said and calmly got dressed and sat back and sipped his coffee.

"Holy moses, mama mia. I've never seen a stud like you before. You're really out to hustle, and boy, oh boy, with what you got, you've got what to hustle with too. I knew you were hung, but boy, are *you* hung!"

Rick merely sipped his coffee and leaned back in his chair, his bulge prominent and bursting at his crotch.

"You've had any acting experience?" Catling asked.

"None. But I learn fast."

"Where you from? Go to school? College?"

"Walt, don't ask about my past. I'm young, healthy, hung, damn attractive. I turn people on, both guys and dolls. Try me by giving me a role. If I'm not good, kick me out on my ass. No hard feelings. I've got to get this movie business out of my system."

"Okay, Rick, I'll level with you. I'm from the Village, Greenwich Village, New York. I've been here for six years now, six long years. I have written many books, many plays, of course, not one of them has been published. I've now written a play, a terrific play, a play about teenagers. It's damned good, I know it, I can feel it. So I want to make a movie based on it, but I want to direct it also. I want no jazzed up version with some rock-and-roll singer in twisting ecstasies. No one in Hollywood will buy my idea, I mean none of the big studios, so I've had to do everything from scratch, get the money, the actors, find the cameramen, the works . . ."

"But what about all the contacts you have?" Rick interrupted.

"What contacts?"

"I mean you surely know big shots to get to all those parties?"

"I crash them. I'm writing another novel about Hollywood so I go to these parties to soak up the atmosphere. I've got a scientific technique of crashing these parties. You see, first . . ."

Rick interrupted him. "Never mind that. Tell me about the movie. Is it going to happen or is it not?"

"It has happened."

"What?"

"The movie will roll. Here," Catling said handing Rick a telegram that read, "I got the moola, flying in Thursday. Bud." Rick read, and asked, "Who's Bud?"

"Bud's my pal. A great guy. He'll be here tomorrow. Then we go to work."

"Congratulations. Do I get a chance?" Rick asked.

"Of course. Now do you believe me?"

"Maybe."

"Maybe!?"

"I've been screwed so many times with promises, I have to be very cautious," Rick said.

"This is definite, kid."

"What's the name of your movie?"

"*Rootless.*"

"Ah, *Rootless*. Rick Talbot in *Rootless*," said Rick, closing his eyes and visualizing a movie marquee.

"That's where you are wrong. There's going to be no star billing for anyone in this movie. Everyone is equal. It will just proclaim the film, *Rootless,* with Rick, Dave, Conrad, and so on. No last names either," said Catling.

"Don't tell me there's going to be no faces either in the movie. Walt, you sure are a crazy writer and director," said Rick.

"How do you photograph?" Catling asked.

"I don't know. I got a good face, a super body, so I ought to look well on screen," Rick said.

"It's not that simple. There are some very handsome people that look positively disgusting in photographs. There are some who are very photogenic. Hope you are that kind."

"I hope so too. But you have so many angles and excuses. You'll suck my cock, snap my photo, and then say, sorry, Rick, you don't photograph well," said Rick.

"Well, let's first photograph you," said Catling.

"I'm glad to hear that at least I'll get that far."

"I'm sure you'll get further. Okay, let's have some action," said

Catling getting up.

"Not until I see the cameras rolling," said Rick and stood up. Catling hugged Rick and cupped his crotch with his palm.

"Big, right?" Rick asked.

"Oh, baby . . ." Catling moaned trying to hug Rick tight. Rick released himself. "Tomorrow, after I'm photographed. Okay?" he said and headed for the door.

"Cockteaser," Catling said.

Rick smiled and left.

22

"ROOTLESS" HAD A BUDGET of fifty thousand dollars, a cast of thirteen actors: eight young men and five young girls. There was no make-up artist, for Catling was against any kind of make-up for young people. No costume designer, for the actors wore well used dungarees, T-shirts, swim trunks, bikinis, and sailor pants. The girls wore trench coats and sweaters. They were bought from Salvation Army and Goodwill and other thrift shops. Nancy, a red-haired girl, was quick with scissors and imagination and made some very creative alterations in the clothes.

The crew was cut to the bone, for Catling was both script writer, director and joint producer with Bud, who served as cameraman and editor.

Rootless dealt with a single day in the lives of thirteen young people, ranging in ages from seventeen to twenty three. They were all physically attractive young people. They exuded vitality and athletic vigor. But each one of them also had an aura of rootlessness, of not belonging, of being the permanent outsider. Bud and Catling had obviously spent several months in picking this group.

The scenes were shot outdoors, and on a single day, in and around Los Angeles.

But there had been plenty of preplanning. The thirteen actors got a four-hour briefing in the small and crowded apartment of Walt Catling. None of the thirteen knew each other. Strangers, they were indifferent to each other, personally and socially. Rick was impressed with Catling, his precision, his meticulous attention to detail, his professionalism. Never had he thought that this fellow, who appeared to be half-drunk in the car parking lot, could be so clear-headed and creative.

"We don't have money to throw around. Everything has to come right the first time. Remember that! Concentrate. Go to your places, think over what I've said, the lines, the moods, and we meet here tomorrow at seven, right on the dot," said Catling.

Nancy read out the outfit each had to wear, and the actors dispersed.

Telling Tom that he had accidentally run into one of his old high school teachers, who had asked all kinds of questions, and whom he had to calm down, Rick managed to take the day off for shooting *Rootless*.

Rick's part was relatively small, but he thought about it all night. He had no lines to say, none at all. "Everything is in your facial expression. Your body language," Catling had instructed him. Bud had suggested a close-up of Rick's face, a privilege none of the other actors had been given.

Under Catling's command as director, the filming went on as scheduled the following day. The entire crew returned to Westwood around ten at night. Everyone was dog tired and without too much ceremony they all dispersed.

"Can you pay me tomorrow?" Catling asked Rick, taking him to one side.

"Pay?"

"Let me suck your superb tool," Catling said.

"Of course. Tomorrow evening, around eight. I'll pay in full. Okay?"

"I'll be waiting."

"Thanks, Walt," said Rick and Catling smiled and watched Rick's magnificent physique move with superb motion under the thin cotton shirt and the tight soft well worn levis.

23

THE FILMING OF *Rootless* had happened so fast, now it was utterly over. No one seemed to know what would happen to it. Rick got no money for his role nor did he experience any special euphoria he had expected to feel after being in a movie.

Now what? Rick wondered. Catling had told him that it would take at least another two months or even more before *Rootless* would be released. He and Bud wanted the musical score for the movie done by a fellow they had both met a few years ago in New Orleans, and seen again in some cafe in the Village. Now they wanted to search him out. He alone, they decided, could do justice to the mood, the tempo, the quivering excitement of *Rootless*. They had heard he was somewhere on Fire Island, on the East Coast, and that's where they were going.

Rick just had to wait.

It seemed to be a dead-end again, except that Rick had a place to stay now, and food to eat, and clothes to wear. Since Eddie had to get some regular physical therapy for his slowly healing hip, and since it was more convenient to have it in Beverly Hills than in the desert house, Tom had decided to stay on. They had paid a year's rent anyway.

Tom began to retreat into silence, began to read voraciously, and stayed home. But Rick felt free to go out, for Tom did not question him, and even encouraged Rick to go out, get a tan, jog by the beach, work out in the gym. As the weeks passed, Rick one day noticed Tom chatting with a bearded, elderly man, wearing a turban. Eddie told Rick that the stranger was a Hindu swami Tom had turned to for peace of mind.

Things were getting crazier, thought Rick, but he feared that one day he would return home and find Tom in some crazy monastic retreat dancing to the tune of a holy man. And then where would Rick be? Out in the streets again? It could very well happen, thought Rick, and began to be concerned.

He called up Mike Snow and briefly told him that he was available. Mike was glad, and when Rick tried to bring him up to date about Tom, Mike said, "I know, Rick, I know."

Rick returned to the gym to work out regularly. He decided to take each day as it came, build his body, and save whatever money he could from delivering champagne for Mike Snow. He was approached by some photographers in the gym asking him to pose for some beefcake pictures. Rick declined.

At the gym, Rick got a shot in the adrenal when others watched him with admiration. Some older men made approaches offering money, but Rick turned them down. What Rick needed was a young hunk, strong and hung, he could fuck. His sex drive was at its peak because Tom had made no demands on him.

A young slim supple-bodied boy by the name of Dave who worked in the gym attracted Rick. He became friendly with him, and visited Dave's home a couple of times, becoming friendly with his parents. But Dave was very shy, and Rick found Dave very attractive and unable to control himself. Rick made the move, one evening, while they were chatting in Dave's room. Dave responded, confessing that Rick was his first sexual experience. Initiating Dave into gay love proved to be an even greater thrill for Rick.

Dave's seduction brought a new dimension of thrill to Rick's life. He had enjoyed the innocence and rapture of Dave, the special throb of sex, and wanted to repeat this experience with other young new gays.

About nearly a month later, Rick again wanted Dave's body and in the gym when they met, Rick whispered, "Dave, I'm hot for you, baby." Dave responded. When they came out of the gym, Dave said that because they had relatives visiting, they would be unable to go to his house. He suggested going to Rick's home. When Rick declined, Dave mildly accused Rick of keeping his life very private. "You know where I live, you know my parents. But I know nothing about you."

"We'll discuss personal lives some other time. Right now I want to slip my cock up your tight sweet ass," Rick said.

"Boy, you sure must be hot."

"I'll show you how hot I am the moment we find a place where we can strip. Besides, you look particularly sexy with your new short haircut," said Rick passing his finger over the smooth shaved nape of Dave's neck.

They drove around for some time, Rick mumbling curses.

"I know what," said Dave.

"What?"

"Let's go to . . ."

"A drive-in," Rick interrupted.

"I was thinking the same," said Dave.

They headed for a drive-in. As they drove up to the cashier of the first drive-in they came across, Dave asked, "I wonder what's playing. I never even saw the board outside."

"Who cares what's playing?" Rick said spreading his thighs.

But as they bought the ticket, Dave asked, "What's playing?"

The man smiled and said, "*Gazebo* and *Rootless*.'

Dave started to pull away, but Rick shouted, "Stop! What did you say?" he asked the man at the counter.

"I told you. *Gazebo* with Debbie Reynolds, and *Rootless* with I don't know who."

"Are you certain?" Rick asked.

"You'll soon find out. Move on, please," the man said.

"What's on now?"

"*Gazebo*"

"And *Rootless*?"

"In another hour. Move on, mister, there's another car behind you," said the man.

"My God, what happened? This sudden interest in the movies?" asked Dave.

"Dave, I can't see the movie. I can't. Let's get out of here, keep driving and come back in an hour. I've got to keep moving. God, I can't sit still," Rick said restlessly.

Dave parked the car, and didn't pick up the speakers. "Hey, what's happened?" he asked Rick, holding him.

Turning around, not caring who was watching him, Rick pulled Dave and kissed him hard. "Come on, let's go. Come on," he urged.

"God, you're crazy," said Dave, but turned the car and came out of the drive-in. "Where do we go now?" he asked after they got on the road.

"I got an idea. Let's go to a movie theatre where the same movies are being shown. There must be another one, because it has to be a multiple release. No, wait a minute, stop near that corner over there," Rick directed.

"Will you tell me what this is all about?" Dave asked.

"In a minute, in a minute," said Rick. "Hey let me have an *Examiner*, will you?" he asked a fellow who was selling newspapers on the corner. "Give me a dime, will you?" he asked, taking the paper and quickly turning to the movie section. Dave paid, and turned the car into the street corner and parked, watching the excited face of Rick.

"I thought so, here," Rick said showing the large advertisement of *Gazebo* and *Rootless* with a big headline saying CITY-WIDE RELEASE OF TWO FILMS.

"So what? I still don't understand all your strange behavior," said Dave.

"Read this, you dope, read," said Rick, pointing to the section dealing with *Rootless*.

"*Rootless*, an explosive film of today's teenagers, to thrill you every minute, featuring the stars of tomorrow. A Sam Steiner release," read Dave. "So?" he questioned.

"I'm in *that* movie!" said Rick.

"You're kidding," Dave said.

"No. I'm not. Let's go and see. That's why I didn't want to see it in a drive-in. It's much more impressive to see it in a theatre," said Rick. "At least for the first time."

"You mean you're a movie star. Really?"

"Let's go and find out," said Rick.

"Gosh, Rick," Dave said, squeezing Rick's biceps.

"Why the hell didn't they tell me that the film was being released?" Rick said as they drove. "Where the hell is Walt?"

"Who is Walt?"

"He's the director, and just about everything else in this film."

"Rick, please calm down. Tell me something more, will you, so that I understand what you're talking about," said Dave.

"I'm sorry, Dave," said Rick stroking Dave's shaved smooth nape. He then briefly told Dave about his debut in *Rootless*. "I've been in a lot of plays in New York. That's where I'm from," Rick said.

"I knew you were a movie stud. I really knew it, the moment I laid eyes on you in the gym," said Dave fueling Rick's ego.

"Really?"

"You couldn't fool me. You're handsome, Rick, you are. And that body, and to add to that, that cock. I tell you, am I lucky to have got fucked by a movie star," Dave said with enthusiasm.

Rick was on cloud nine with these comments by Dave.

They drove on and finally spotted a movie house where both the films were being shown. They parked the car and Dave bought the tickets, and they entered the theatre.

"In another twenty minutes," the man said in answer to Rick's question concerning the showing of *Rootless*.

The theatre was fairly crowded, but Rick and Dave sat close to the aisle. Rick kept wishing the other movie would hurry up and end. Then there was a brief intermission and then *Rootless* flashed on the screen.

The musical background and the theme song of *Rootless* had a haunting, disturbing quality. The audience seemed to like it. One of the girls behind Rick said to her boyfriend, "I'm going to buy this record." Then came the credits, set against a dry desert background. "With," the cast read, and Rick whispered, "Watch carefully." The names came, brief, precise, in big bold letters, just the first names: Conrad, Danny, the alphabetical list was approaching closer, Kenny . . . Peter and Rick. Dave clasped Rick's hand. Rick grasped it tightly and held his breath.

They kept watching, the movie started. The audience seemed spellbound. There was a hushed silence as the drama unfolded. Ah, there he was now, Rick himself, in a seductively torn shirt showing off his pecs and one nipple. His tight dungarees were patched at the butt and torn at the knees. Dark haired, his hair tantalizingly wind-blown, he sat on a garbage can staring vacantly into space. He slowly lifted his face, shook his head to brush back the hair, and the camera moved close for a full picture of his virile face. "Gosh, I'm ready to cream in my pants. You look great," Dave whispered. Then the camera turned on someone else, for in this scene by the beach all the thirteen rootless persons were shown, one after the other.

The movie rolled on, with a tempo and an athletic vigor that captivated the audience, and again Rick whispered, "I think I come on now. Watch." He was on the screen again in the same outfit, except that his shirt was off and thus showed off his broad muscular bronzed chest. He comes ambling onto the beach. He has been hurt. He tries to communicate, but his lips barely move. He falls on the sand writhing in pain. The crowd surrounds him and a girl kneels to gently cradle his body on her lap. The camera catches Rick's full face, intensely alive in sheer agony, and lingers on his bare chest and on his sweat-covered forehead and on his lips. Watching his handsomeness Rick felt a warm shock of pleasure and excitement. The theatre echoed squeals of approval from the girls in the audience, and Rick heard a boy in the back row cry out, "What a stud" in an effeminate voice.

When it ended, and the lights came on, Dave and Rick came out with the crowd, and Rick was delighted to hear comments. "That was terrific, never expected that." "What a bunch of hunks, everyone so gorgeous," said a girl. "I liked the guy who died. I sure dig him," added another. Rick for a moment wanted to say, "Hey, I'm that hunk."

They returned to the car. Dave praised Rick, admired him, said passionate things. But Rick was in a dream world, still finding it hard to believe that he was indeed in a movie.

"What's next? How can I get in touch with Walt? Maybe there are guys looking for me for other roles," lamented Rick.

Dave tried to calm him, promising him the best blow job he'd ever had. He suggested that they spend the night together by renting a motel or hotel room.

Rick wanted to see the movie again, just *Rootless*, and they drove around for some time, and went to a drive-in restaurant, but Rick was too excited to eat. They left, to return to the theatre. Dave called home to say that he was not coming home that night and not to worry. They entered the theatre to watch *Rootless* one more time.

Rick admired his face and body once again, thrilled again by the favorable comments by the audience, heard Dave's unrestrained admiration and then they both drove to the Y to get a double room.

Dave offered himself to Rick, and Rick ploughed him to sheer ecstasy.

24

THEY WOKE UP EARLY when the maid knocked on the door to say it was check out time. "We'll be out soon," shouted Rick and playfully hit Dave on his naked butt and said, "Get up, boy, get up. Time to rise and shine."

They showered together, and since they were the only two in the shower, they horsed around and Rick had a glorious erection. Dave hungrily fell to the floor and sucked out Rick's cream.

They checked out, had breakfast, and Rick said, "I think I'll see you later, Dave. I have to go to Beverly Hills to see a friend."

"Rick, you mind if I come with you?" Dave asked.

"Where to?"

"Wherever you go. You're a star, or soon will be one. I'll be your valet, servant, bodyguard, gofer, slave, whatever you want."

The offer surprised Rick.

"Thanks, Dave. But I'm hardly the kind of star who can afford such service."

"Why?"

"Listen, Dave, I can't have someone like you with me. What'll we do for money? It's no use even talking about it. Anyway, let's wait. Okay? I'm not going to run off," Rick said.

"But I love you, Rick. I do. You're the only one with whom I've had sex. And I'll keep it that way. It was you who brought me out, remember?"

"Yes, I remember. But listen, I'll call you later this evening, and we'll talk about it. Okay?"

Dave drove Rick towards Beverly Hills, and long before reaching Tom's home, Rick got out of the car. Dave drove away reluctantly, and only after extracting several promises from Rick that he would call him later that day.

Rick walked slowly. He did not exactly know what he was going to do. One thing was certain, he had to stay with Tom till Catling made contact with him. He wondered if he ought to discuss his next move with Tom in a circuitous way, one of those "doctor, my friend is pregnant, I need some advice" routines. But decided not to risk Tom's jealousy. Anyway he felt happy at the way he had come off in the movie, sexy and attractive, although he had not even uttered a line.

As he turned the corner to get into the house, he saw a sports car parked on the curb, and immediately recognized it as Dick Darrah's. "Oh, no," thought Rick, "Tom is trying to make another come-back."

As he approached the house, he noticed that Darrah was sitting in the car. He came out the moment he saw Rick, smiled, and said, "Ah, the young star," and offered his hand.

Rick shook hands.

"Come, sit down, get in," Dick said pointing to the car.

"I have to go in," said Rick.

"That, my friend, is your past," Dick said dramatically, and pointing to the car said, "This is your future. Come on, get in. I've been waiting for you since early morning."

He opened the car door and Rick got in. Then Dick started to drive.

"Congratulations. You made it," said Dick.

"Well, thanks. But just one movie, not even a dialogue," said Rick.

"You are modest. I like it."

"So you saw the movie and recognized me?"

"Better than that. I got a look at your sneak preview reactions."

"Where was that?"

"In New York. My talent scout called me to give me the report. Seventy-two percent of the audience mentioned you, not by name, for no one knows your name, but called you "the handsome hunk who got killed," "handsome muscle kid." Poor Conrad was the star, although there was supposed to *be* no star in *Rootless*. Am I right?"

"Yeah, that's right. That's what Walt said."

"Ah, Walt Catling, the magnificent eccentric. Anyway Conrad did get mentioned a couple of times, but you, Rick, you topped the survey numbers. Not a word from you, yet your face has launched a thousand fan clubs," said Dick with great excitement.

"Fan clubs?"

"Amazing, isn't it? Here you are, like thousands of other young men, wanting to get into a movie. You got the break, a small one, the smallest. Then bingo, without your knowledge, your face and body are lighting a small fire. Girls are hot for you, and men too, to be quite frank."

"How do you know all this?"

Dick pulled over at a dead-end road, lighted a cigarette and said, "Rick, I'd like to handle you. Of course right now you're a hot property. There'll be quite a few who'll be eager to represent you. They'll get you a few fast movies, you know, the teenage troubled youth rumble type, to show off your naked chest and body. You'll be stereotyped and then wham, it's all over. But I will and I can handle you properly. Get you the right type of roles. I'm a good agent. I can take you to the top."

"Why do you say that?"

"I'll tell you why. You have not proved anything else in this movie except that you photograph beautifully. You reveal a splendid animal vigor. You are a very sexy stud, and you project that sex onto film. In fact you look sexier on film than in real life. You are sexy, don't mistake me, but on camera you intensify that quality. I noticed you in the desert house, you wanted to be noticed. Nothing wrong with that. I said to myself, this kid knows how to hustle. Twice you quietly paraded in front of me, by the pool in your tight white stretch bikini. Oh, yes, I noticed every move you made. Without anyone telling me, I knew your relationship with Tom. Any fool would have known that you were Tom's kept boy. You were just biding your time to get a break."

"But, Dick, if you knew I was gay, why did you ask Tom if he were gay?"

"Simple. After I took Tom as a client, I knew he was washed out. I wanted to dump him. I used that as an excuse. I'm not against gays. I don't give a damn if a guy screws a woman or a boy, as long as he's got talent I can smell. You got it," said Dick matter-of-factly.

"So I have talent, huh?" Rick asked.

"Well, yes, but it's got to be shaped, disciplined. But you have to select the right agent to handle you, if not they'll squeeze you dry in a couple of years, and you'll end up like Tom Shane."

"Who's 'they'?"

"Agents, publicity men, all the other vultures in this business who want to make big bucks very fast."

"Don't tell me you're going to tote me free of charge. All for love or for sex?"

"Not for sex, my friend. You don't have to worry about that part. I'm a pussy fucker all the way. But I'll take my commission just like everyone else, except that I'll take it easy, look for the long term investment."

"I can hardly believe that it's happened, that I'm talking to a hot shot agent like you," said Rick.

"It has happened. But if you're not careful, it can be over very fast too," said Dick Darrah.

"What's my next move?"

"To sign some papers to legalize that I'm your agent. By the way how old are you?"

"Around twenty-two."

"Good. That makes you legally responsible."

"What next after signing these papers?"

"I'll get you a nice but small place to stay, keep you sort of isolated, and in the meanwhile we'll launch a big publicity blitz to create a demand for you."

"But I want to stop and see Tom before I come with you."

"Why?"

"To pick up my clothes. I have quite a load. I like them, particularly the ones I bought in Rome."

"Okay, But make it fast, no dilly-dallying or sweet, sentimental goodbyes. No last minute quickie blow job for Mr. Queer . . ."

"Cut that out!" Rick snapped at him. "He's a good man. No need to kick him when he's down and out," said Rick.

"Sorry, Rick. I admire your loyalty. I mean that sincerely," said Dick Darrah.

They drove back to Tom's home. Dick dropped Rick off and said he'd return in an hour with a bigger car to transport Rick's belongings.

Eddie was not home when Rick entered Tom's home. Tom was lounging on the couch with an unshaven face and wearing his pyjamas. He had been drinking.

"I'm sorry about last night, Rick, real sorry," said Tom.

Rick did not know what he was talking about. He wanted to ask, but did not. He just said, "That's okay, Tom, we all make mistakes."

"Oh, Rick, how sweet you are," Tom said and lunged forward to hug Rick and kiss him. Rick gave him a casual hug, but pulled away when Tom wanted to kiss him. The smell of liquor on Tom's breath disgusted him.

"Where's Eddie?" Rick asked.

"Gone for his therapy. Poor Eddie. Poor faithful Eddie, poor sweet Rick, my best buddies. My two best damn good buddies in this whole fucking world," Tom said.

Rick went to his room, locked the door, and started to pack. Those he couldn't fit into the two large suitcases, he brought down on hangers into the living room. "Lots of clothes to get cleaned, Tom. I'm taking them to the dry cleaning place," he said by way of explanation. But Tom did not seem to care what Rick was doing.

Rick brought all the stuff out onto the porch and waited, hoping that Dick Darrah would show up before Eddie returned from his therapy. He did not want to face Eddie with the truth.

Dick Darrah pulled up and helped Rick with his belongings. Hearing the sound of the car, Tom cried out from inside, "Eddie? Eddie, is that you?"

Even as Tom managed to come to the door, Rick drove away in Dick Darrah's car without looking back, but rather looking forward to his new life.

25

I T WAS A COMFORTABLE SUITE of rooms in a small but exclusive hotel in Pasadena where Rick was asked to stay by Dick Darrah. "Restrict your movements, watch TV, go to a late show if you want to, but above all keep your mouth shut. I'll send you all the newspapers to keep you informed about how the public is howling for you. When it reaches the right crescendo, then I'll introduce you. Okay?" Dick Darrah said, patting Rick on the back.

As Rick followed the papers, he thrilled at the way Dick Darrah was orchestrating Rick's importance. The theatres where *Rootless* had been shown had been bombarded with hundreds of letters from fans asking that their letters be forwarded to "the Cute boy;" "The Swell kid;" "The Hunk;" and so on, care of the director of *Rootless,* care of the name of the theatre where the movie was being shown. It was as though the whole cast of *Rootless* had disbanded without a trace. It had really happened that way too. Bud and Catling had fallen out, the Black musician who had composed the haunting and arresting music for the film had been busted on a drug charge. Bud had impregnated the redheaded girl in the cast, and Conrad had been propositioned by Catling and got beaten as a result. They had run out of money, and sold the entire movie rights for release, distribution and what-not to Sam Steiner.

But the movie after release had created quite an impression. It had been praised by even the sternest critics for its artistic integrity and originality.

Conrad had already cashed in, as, Rick noted from the papers, by accepting quite a few TV roles, and had said that he knew nothing about the whereabouts of Rick, not even his full name. He had issued a statement.

But still the question in the press and on TV was: who is this handsome actor who had received one of the largest fan mails, although he had not spoken a single line?

Rick wanted to go out on the street, but disciplined himself to follow Dick Darrah's suggestion and stay isolated. He felt bored, of course, being by himself in the hotel, watching TV and eating. He wanted to go out in the sun, exercise, run free on the beach, swim, make love. He could not control himself any longer. So he called Dave, who raced over, and submitted his young pliant body to Rick's aroused domination.

"You're the talk of the town, Rick," said Dave. "Boy, am I lucky to see you, be your buddy, suck your thick meat. Oh, boy, am I lucky," Dave repeated over and over again.

"Keep your mouth shut, though. Not a word of this to anyone," Rick instructed.

"Oh, Rick, I wouldn't do anything without your permission," Dave assured him.

About two weeks later, Dick Darrah came over and said, "Well, Rick, tomorrow you are going to face the eager world. Jonathan Studios has agreed to give you a contract for three years and . . . well, don't worry your head with all the details. But it's a terrific contract. We'll both get rich. Now listen," Dick Darrah said and started telling Rick what he should do at the studio the next morning when they would meet the big shots, and what he should and should not say at the press conference.

"Dick, I'm nervous," said Rick.

"Well, it's your first acting experience. You'll be in the spot light. We'll go through the procedure again. I'll coach you," Dick assured him.

Dick kept his promise, returned later and coached Rick meticulously. He provided Rick with a set of biographical facts about his past life, enough to make him respectable, create the image of a sort of Horatio Alger story. He asked Rick to dress very casually in well laundered Levis, a pair of sneakers, a button down blue Oxford, and a Navy blue cashmere crew neck sweater.

They drove to the studio at lunch time, driving through the large iron gates after the man at the entrance had called to make sure that Mr. Darrah and Mr. Rick Talbot had an appointment. "Next time you come in, Rick," Dick said driving in, "these gates will swing open the minute your car is spotted."

They were ushered into the inner chamber where four men presided over the vast celluloid empire of the studio. All the four rose to greet Dick Darrah and Rick. They smiled broadly indicating that they were pleased with the commodity they had purchased, namely Rick.

A stocky gentleman in gray was the first to speak. "Dick, Mr. Talbot is definitely a good-looker. Very clean cut, very wholesome. Mr. Talbot, or Rick, if I may call you, I hope our relationship will be long and very rewarding."

"Thank you, sir," said Rick shaking hands.

"See those six photos of six young men, Rick," the man said pointing to the wooden panel in the room. "These six young men are the hottest stars of today, but we will make you top all of them," he said and gripped Rick's shoulder.

Following the instructions that Dick had given, Rick merely smiled.

"We understand that Mr. Darrah has been your friend and mentor for a very long time."

"Yes, I owe everything to Mr. Darrah," Rick said.

They chitchatted a bit more, then had lunch in the luxurious executive dining room. A studio photographer appeared and took several photos of Rick, just his face from several angles. By the time lunch was over, the photographer had returned with prints of all the photos he had taken. Rick fell in love with his photos. Everyone joined in carefully selecting the picture that was most appealing. "It's a hard job," said the photographer. "He is one of the most photogenic young men I've ever photographed," he added to Rick's great joy.

Finally two prints were selected and fifty copies of each were ordered, so that they could be handed out to the newsmen at the press conference.

Rick was given a guided tour of the studio, and then ushered into the large, air-conditioned lounge to meet the reporters. Rick was nervous, and Dick Darrah gently patted him on the back and said, "Relax, smile a lot and you'll slay them."

Flash bulbs popped, and reporters crowded towards him. After some order had been restored, a slim young man from the press and public relations department of the studio introduced Rick, "the new young star who will set the film world ablaze with his talent."

Then the questions came, and Rick was hesitant at first, but gradually got into the spirit of the show. Although this was his first press conference, he had scripted this fantasy so many times in his mind that he had no difficulty in acting out this reality.

Dick Darrah and the studio bosses were grinning from ear to ear at Rick's masterly handling of the press. But there was a sudden entry into the lounge of an elderly lady that brought with her a sense of heightened tension. A few of the studio chiefs got up deferentially, and a few reporters as well. This was Lydia Lester, referred to in movie circles as Hollywood's Number One Hatchet Woman. Lydia was a powerful gossip columnist, whose column about the doings of the stars was featured in hundreds of newspapers across the country. To be mentioned in her column was the desire of all stars, and she could make, mend, or end many a movie career. She always wanted the first scoop on anything and everything dealing with the movie world, from abortions to assasinations. For weeks she had tried to get the scoop on Rick, the mystery star, but had failed.

"So this is the boy you've kept under cover, Grant," she said, addressing the studio cheif in gray, and looking at Rick.

"It is a rare pleasure to meet you, Miss Lester," Rick said, smiling and very courteously.

Lydia was taken aback, but she offered her hand.

"I've always read your column. So did my mother. In a sense it was because of your column that I got inspired to set my goals on Hollywood," Rick said, pouring it on thick.

Lydia was charmed. Rick was not lying when he said that he had always read her column. He had even when he was in Clinton.

"Grant, this boy pours it on thick, doesn't he? But I like it," Lydia said, pleased with the position she had now acquired as the center of attraction. "Come on, let's sit and talk," she said, going towards a sofa, where those who were sitting got up to make room for her. The photographers snapped Rick and Lydia, and Grant and Dick Darrah beamed in satisfaction at the way things had turned out.

Dick Darrah had promised Rick one of the biggest publicity moves, and he had succeeded, for Rick's picture stared from every newspaper, most magazine covers, and parts of the press conference were on TV. Rick was elated beyond description. He was briefly disturbed by the thought as to what would happen if his innumerable anonymous and not so anonymous lovers were to recognize his face. Well, what if they did? If anyone took the trouble to expose him, it would only create a juicy publicity scandal. Besides most of the guys would probably rather look at his photo and jack off, than sit and write a letter. Who cares, anyway, he said to himself, and began to look at the papers and magazines containing his photos.

26

I T HAD BEEN A GRUELING SIX MONTHS of hard work, parties, publicity, continuous travel from one hick town to another. Rick was being sold from every possible angle as the new heart throb, so that his first full length movie *I Want to Say Something* in glorious technicolor, cinemascope and stereophonic music would be the biggest box office hit of the year!

Rick had enjoyed every minute of it, the attention by screaming crowds of youngsters and even older folks. Now the publicity tour was almost at an end. He had also seen the rushes and the full movie in a darkened movie house at a sneak preview. Audience reaction had been splendid. The grand premiere was set to take place at the Egyptian Theatre on Hollywood Boulevard. Rick was to escort Angelina Atwater, the bright new starlet, to the premiere. He had already been photographed with her in very lovey dovey poses in places from Villa Capri to Sunset Boulevard.

There were three more stops to go, and then L.A. for the big premiere. Then he had planned at least three months of total relaxation either in Hawaii or the Bahamas or even maybe Rome.

But as he stepped out of the shower that evening, in the best hotel that Oshkosh, Wisconsin could provide, Rick felt an overwhelming sense of loneliness. Crowds of hysterical teenagers had been orchestrated by Dick Darrah wherever Rick had traveled, from one small town to another. In fact Rick could even now, as he dried himself, hear the voices and laughter of youngsters beneath his window. There was the faint cry of "we want Rick," as though they were rehearsing, preparing to shout even louder as soon as Dick Darrah brought in the media. After the media had got enough photos, Darrah would chase the kids away.

That Dick Darrah! Just an efficient, cold-hearted son of a bitch,

Rick thought. Did the man have any human emotions? He always talked about packaging Rick properly to be sold as a commodity. How unceremoniously he had told Dave to get lost. "You get rid of your queer buddy," he had ordered Rick. "He's turned into a disgusting little prancing fairy. He'll ruin your wholesome image. He'll ruin my investment in you." When Rick had attempted to defend Dave, Dick Darrah had interrupted him in the same no-nonsense manner. "Listen, Rick, do your fucking and sucking behind closed doors after we complete this tour, when we reach L.A." So Dave had left.

Since then there had developed an air of uneasy tension between Dick Darrah and Rick.

Rick missed Dave. As he put on his pale blue silk robe, he decided that when he reached L.A. he would try to track down Dave and have him come and live with him. Rick missed the company of Eddie too, the wise, protective, fatherly Eddie. He missed Turk who had really been his friend, who had helped motivate Rick to build up a superb body and also train his mind. Turk was intelligent too. He wished he knew where Turk was and made another resolution to track him down as well when he reached L.A.

Rick felt he couldn't trust Dick Darrah. Not having anyone he could trust, anyone with whom he could confide, increased Rick's sense of loneliness.

Rick felt restless for not being able to satisfy his sexual hunger. There were many priapic young men whom Rick had spotted in the crowds, who would have gladly submitted to his desires, but Dick Darrah had watched him like a hawk and would permit no quickie one night stand. Besides, Rick did not really know if he wanted any more one night stands.

Rick missed the warm sun, the stretch of sandy beach, the vigorous swim and the pain and pleasure of working up a sweat in the gym. This life of the celebrity was not what it was all cracked up to be, he thought.

He ordered room service and had his dinner, watched some TV and went to bed.

Next morning Dick Darrah announced that the two stopovers had been cancelled. Rick was overjoyed.

"Don't you even want to know the reason?" Darrah asked.

"I'm sure they're good. I trust your judgment," Rick replied, happy that they would fly back to L.A.

They drove to Chicago to catch the flight to Los Angeles. Their flight had been delayed and Darrah closeted himself in a phone booth to make his innumerable calls. Rick browsed in the newstand area and bought the California papers. It was while he was looking through the San Francisco *Chronicle* that he saw a picture that made him sit up. The picture was about the opening of a record store on Polk Street. In the picture was Turk! It was his store and the story went on to say that it was one of the few openly gay businesses in the city. Turk Corbin's Music Store was Turk's way of coming out. Rick could hardly contain his joy at having found out where Turk was. He wondered for a second what Turk would say if he called him. Best way is to find out, he decided and hastened to a phone booth.

He dialled and asked for information and called the Music Store. A young man answered, and Rick asked to speak to Turk. A few seconds later Turk came on.

"Turk, this is Rick."

There was a pause at the other end.

"Turk, are you there?"

"Yes, I'm here. How are you, Rick?"

"Oh, Turk. Am I glad to hear your voice. Am I glad to locate you. I just picked up this newspaper and . . ." Rick poured out his words, his emotions, his joy at discovering Turk again.

Easy, Rick. Easy. I've been reading about you too. Big star and all that."

"But Turk, please, will you forgive me."

"There's nothing to forgive, Rick."

"Oh, there is, Turk. I'll make it up to you. I'll help you with your record business. I got money. We can live together, be friends again. I'm going to get myself a nice home. I'll even move to San Francisco . . ."

"Rick, hold it. Take it easy. Let's get reacquainted before you make all these big plans."

"Are you politely telling me to get lost?"

"Oh, Rick, I would never do that. Do you know how many times I wanted to get in touch with you?"

"Why didn't you?"

"Well, you were a celebrity . . ."

"Oh, I've had enough of being a celebrity."

"I suppose you say that because you're weary from all your publicity travels! You see, I've been following you!"

"I'm flattered. Turk, I owe you an apology . . ."

"Rick, the past is the past. By the way, where are you now?"

"I told you. In the Chicago airport, on my way to L.A. I can just as well fly to San Francisco, if you want to."

"That's sweet of you, Rick. No, you go on to L.A. Get settled and give me a call. We'll meet . . ."

"You'll fly over to L.A.?"

"I will, if you want me to."

"Of course I want you to. I really missed you, Turk."

"I did too, Rick. I'm still hoping to see you in all your naked splendor."

"Oh, baby, I'm going to put on a strip show for you that you'll never forget."

There was a knocking on the phone booth door. It was Dick Darrah pointing to his watch and asking Rick to hurry up.

"Turk, look, I gotta go. But, please, Turk, please don't ever abandon me."

"I won't."

"I love you."

"I love you, too."

Rick hung up and came out with a great big smile.

"What are you suddenly so happy about?" Dick Darrah asked.

"I found a dear sweet friend. But you wouldn't understand, Dick," said Rick and walked briskly towards the lobby to catch his flight to L.A.

Published in paperback. There is also a special edition of ten numbered copies, handbound in boards and signed by the author.